BLINDED BY

Doms of Destiny, Colorado 8

Chloe Lang

MENAGE EVERLASTING

Siren Publishing, Inc.
www.SirenPublishing.com

A SIREN PUBLISHING BOOK
IMPRINT: Ménage Everlasting

BLINDED BY BEAUTY
Copyright © 2014 by Chloe Lang

ISBN: 978-1-62741-767-9

First Printing: August 2014

Cover design by Les Byerley
All art and logo copyright © 2014 by Siren Publishing, Inc.

Printed in the U.S.A.

PUBLISHER
Siren Publishing, Inc.
www.SirenPublishing.com

DEDICATION

It's hard to believe that this is the eighth book in the Doms of Destiny, Colorado series. I continue to fall in love with the people who populate the pages of this town. There are so many to thank but here are just a few I'd like to dedicate this book to:

Lanae Lemore – who kept pushing me to write a book for Jaris. She was an integral part in making this come to fruition.

Chloe Vale – who dots every *i* and crosses every *t* and keeps the commas in the right places in my manuscripts. Without her, I would be lost.

Liz Berry – whose encouragement and upbeat spirit continues to lift me up. She makes me strive to do more.

Sophie Oak – who continues to cheer me on and who helped me conceive of the entire series. She helped me take the idea into a reality.

Shayla Black – who is always ready to listen to me when I need to bounce ideas off her. She is a loving mentor and friend.

BLINDED BY BEAUTY

Doms of Destiny, Colorado 8

CHLOE LANG
Copyright © 2014

Chapter One

A gun fired.

He leapt in front of his former partner, hoping to deflect the bullet from the crazy woman, whose eyes were filled with hate.

He fell to the ground with a thud.

Staring up into the sky, he saw the blue quickly fading to a dark gray.

Then everything went black.

"Am I dead?"

Jaris Simmons's arms and legs got tangled up in his sheets, forcing him back into the consciousness of the darkness that had been his reality since the shooting.

He took a deep, calming breath and swung his legs off the bed. Sugar, his service dog and companion, nuzzled his leg.

Though his heart was still pounding hard in his chest, he patted Sugar on the head. "It's all right, girl. Just a bad dream."

He'd never felt so close to any animal as he felt to her. Before Sugar, the only pet he'd ever had in his life was a turtle when he was a kid. Having lost his vision prior to getting Sugar, he'd never seen what his dog looked like. But he'd been told she was a black German shepherd with one tiny white spot just above her chest.

The door to his room squeaked softly.

"Everything okay?" The question came from a man whose voice Jaris knew better than any other and who had taught him how to adapt and accept his blindness.

Chance Reynolds. They'd only known each other for a little over a year, but even so Chance was most definitely his best friend in the world.

"I'm fine. Sorry if I woke you, buddy."

"It was Annie who heard you. I was in a deep sleep."

Annie was Chance's service dog of many years.

Jaris and Chance had been living at the Boys Ranch, a home for orphans, for a few months. The Stone family had built the place and the good that they did here was impressive. Everyone in Destiny, Colorado, supported the orphan boys with open arms. He liked the town, which was like no other place he'd ever been to. Though he missed his job as a detective back in Chicago, what he and Chance accomplished here with the boys was extremely rewarding. Those little cowboys were helping train Kaylyn Anderson's service dogs. Although Kaylyn loved singing, everyone knew her first priority was her dog training school.

He'd gotten Sugar after she'd graduated from Kaylyn's rigorous instructions. Annie, too, had come from Kaylyn.

Kaylyn and Chance had been working together for years. His friend trained blind individuals and Kaylyn provided each of Chance's students with a service dog. Chance had lived in Denver for many years, but had recently moved to Destiny with Jaris to start working side by side with Kaylyn. The last several months had been some of the best of his life, working with Chance, the dogs, the little cowboys, but especially Kaylyn.

Kaylyn. Why can't I get her out of my mind? Because of her amazing, caring heart and infectious laugh, not to mention her incredible singing voice. Whenever Jaris heard her sing with Wolfe Mayhem, Mitchell Wolfe's band, he would've sworn he was hearing an angel.

He was certain she was beautiful. He'd learned that Kaylyn had long blonde hair and gray eyes after hearing her mother, Betty, bragging about her.

God, if he could get one look at Kaylyn, it would mean the world to him.

Didn't matter. It could never be anything but friendship between them. Nothing more. It was clear to him that she and Chance belonged together. What was holding them back from one another? He still didn't know but was determined to find out.

"Annie, go say good morning to your sister."

Jaris could hear the shuffling of Chance's service dog moving next to Sugar. The two dogs were good together.

"Was it the dream about the shooting again?" Chance asked.

He nodded, but knowing his friend had been blind since birth, added, "Yep."

"Damn, Jaris. That's three times this week." Chance sat on the mattress next to him. "Won't you please go talk to Patrick O'Leary about this?"

"No psychiatrists. It'll pass. Besides, when would I have time? Kaylyn has us on a tight schedule." He didn't mind. There were four blind teenagers around the country anxiously waiting to get their service dogs from Kaylyn's school. The work they were all doing was important.

Chance stood. "You're right about us not having much time. Rex, King, and Blue are close to being ready, but Rosie still needs a little more training since we started with her later."

"Yes, but I'm sure she'll be ready before their new owners arrive. Lyle's been working extra with her." Lyle Barker started working for Kaylyn when he was in high school. Lyle was a good man and clearly someone she felt responsible for.

"Glad he's on our team, but it's still quite the task we have since the whole town has got dragon fever."

"Even Kaylyn is burning up with it." Jaris stood, grabbing Sugar's leash. "She's going to be busy with the festivities. I think her band is performing several times during the week."

He found the quirkiness of Destiny charming, including the fact that some of its citizens actually believed in the existence of dragons. Starting tomorrow was a weeklong event that celebrated that fact. People from around the world attended Dragon Week.

Sheriff Jason Wolfe had deputized almost everyone in town for Dragon Week to ensure public safety, but especially to watch out for Belle.

The town had an enemy still on the loose that had kept everyone on high alert—Kip Lunceford, a killer who was battling leukemia. Kip had declared war on Destiny and vowed to kidnap Belle Blue, wife of Shane and Corey. Turned out that Belle was a bone marrow donor match for Lunceford.

Jaris wasn't surprised that the sheriff hadn't asked him and Chance to take badges. *What good can two blind guys do to keep the peace?* He reached to the nightstand and touched his pistol, which he was never without. He hadn't fired it since losing his sight. That would be dangerous given his blindness. He missed the gun range back in Chicago, a place he visited at least twice a week. Back then he'd been quite the shot.

I guess I have my own quirks to deal with—a blind man carrying a gun. Actually, it's pretty funny when I think about it.

He could hear Sugar and Annie licking each other. It was clear to him that dogs, like humans, had friendships. The perfect example was right at his feet. The bond that existed between Annie and Sugar was unbreakable, just like his friendship with Chance.

He reached down and patted both of the dogs on their heads. "Chance, we better get up and get moving. We need to head down to the kennels before Kaylyn does. We don't want to be late. You know how she is about her schedules."

They both laughed and headed off to get dressed.

* * * *

The March breeze, which was unusually warm for this time of year, felt good on Chance's skin. He stood by the fence with Annie, waiting for Kaylyn to arrive.

Jaris was in the yard with Sugar at his side. The former detective was as solid as they came. Honest. Loyal. Dedicated. A true-blue friend.

Working with Jaris had been the catalyst to all that had happened to Chance the past year. Destiny was home to both of them now.

Jaris and Lyle were directing the boys on how to get the other four dogs in their harnesses.

Lyle was shy and extremely quiet most of the time, but whenever he was around the dogs, the guy was in his element.

The remote training was one of the most important lessons for the canines. Service dogs had to be able to get help when their master was down. This was a big test for Rex, King, Blue, and Rosie.

He heard Jaris and Lyle walk over to him. "Are the four dogs ready for their test?"

"They are," Lyle answered. "I need to go check on Sammie."

Sammie was a Labrador retriever who was due to deliver pups any day. The litter would be the newest class of canines in Kaylyn's school. There were another eight dogs that were at various stages of training that Lyle kept tabs on.

"Go ahead, Lyle," he said, knowing the guy was anxious to check on Sammie. "We've got this."

"Thanks, fellas." Lyle left.

"I hope the boss lady isn't late," Jaris teased. "Her coffee will be cold."

"It's in a thermos, Jaris. You know that." Like he did every morning, Chance had coffee ready for Kaylyn. "Plus, she won't be late and you know it. Kaylyn is as punctual as a Swiss clock." Chance lifted his wrist and punched the button on his watch.

The digital voice announced, "The time is 6:56 a.m."

Jaris laughed. "Four minutes. I don't hear her truck, do you?"

"No, but I have no doubt she'll be here on time." Back when Silver Spoon Bridge had still been under construction and everyone had to use the ferryboats to get in and out of town, Kaylyn hadn't been late a single morning. Now that the bridge was fully operational, she was normally early.

Jaris placed his hand on his shoulder. "Still glad I convinced you to move here?"

"Every day." His life had taken a big change when he'd agreed to relocate to Destiny with Jaris to help Kaylyn with her dog training school. It felt like it was the best decision he'd made in a very long time.

Jaris had come to Denver after being shot and losing his sight. Jaris was a hero. Everyone in Destiny said so, including Kaylyn. Jaris had been the best student he'd ever had, which was saying something since the man had been twenty-nine years old the day he'd arrived at Chance's doorstep. Children typically took to the training better than adults. Jaris was the exception. He was like a sponge, taking in everything, learning to rely on his other senses to adapt to the world around him. But it wasn't just how impressed Chance had been with Jaris's abilities that had bonded them together like brothers.

Jaris was the only student Chance had ever taught—and he'd taught many—who had taken the time to ask him about his own personal struggles with blindness. It had never felt like a struggle to Chance, just a reality he'd always known.

He'd been lucky growing up in a wealthy African-American family. His father had been a lawyer and his mother a surgeon. He loved his parents very much. They never coddled him, pushing him to be all that he could be. When he'd told them about moving to Destiny, they'd been completely supportive. In fact, they had begun donating to Kaylyn's dog training school.

He and Jaris made quite the team at her school. The work they did with dogs and the Boys Ranch orphans had given him much satisfaction. They were producing some very highly trained service dogs that would be helping people around the country.

Moving to Destiny had been the right thing for him for many reasons, but one in particular he held close to his heart.

I get to spend more time with Kaylyn.

Chance punched the button on his watch again.

"The time is 6:58 a.m."

"Two minutes and counting, buddy." The mirth in Jaris's tone was obvious.

"Okay, Detective." He laughed. "I got a nickel in my pocket that says she'll be here on the dot."

"You got a bet."

He and Kaylyn had been friends for many years, working together to help the blind, but his feelings for her had moved beyond friendship.

He'd known for some time that he was in love with her.

Two Christmases ago he'd had too much wine at Kaylyn's mother's holiday party. Inhaling Kaylyn's sweet aroma had ignited his desires. Standing in the doorway together, he'd placed his arm around Kaylyn's shoulder. Someone near them had pointed out that they were under the mistletoe. Courage or foolishness had swept through him. Without thinking, he'd pulled Kaylyn in close and kissed her.

Her response seemed to be complete shock, crushing his hopes. "Wow. Chance, I—"

Realizing he'd overstepped, he released her. "Don't say anything, Kaylyn. I'm sorry. Too much to drink."

He'd left quickly, fearing he had damaged their friendship completely. But he hadn't. The next day they'd gone back to work, talking about his new clients and her new pups but never mentioning what had happened the night before. He'd vowed that day to always keep his feelings for Kaylyn under control.

As much as he wanted to hold her in his arms and kiss her, he was certain the relationship they had would end if he ever told her the truth about how he felt.

He wasn't willing to risk losing Kaylyn.

What they had together would have to be enough. It was absolutely better than not being with her at all.

Annie's tail began wagging, hitting his leg. Her hearing was better than his, and seconds later he could hear the rumble of Kaylyn's truck off in the distance.

"Listen, Jaris. You recognize that sound, don't you?"

"I sure do. Looks like I owe you a nickel."

Chapter Two

Kaylyn stepped out of the truck. She smiled, seeing Chance pouring her usual cup of coffee.

Her feelings for him had been growing for years despite all her efforts to keep them in check. She cared deeply for him. Her mind drifted back to the one kiss they'd shared. *God, how I wish it had meant more to him. It sure meant so much to me.* He'd never given any signs that she was anything other than a friend to him. She'd learned to keep her feelings in check, especially now that he and Jaris were part of her training team.

Jaris and the boys had the dogs harnessed and ready to go.

"Good morning, fellas." She looked up. "This day is perfect. The clouds look like big puffy bales of cotton floating in the sky."

"That's painting a perfect picture for a blind man since birth, sweetheart." Chance smiled, making her weak in the knees. "Thank you."

"You're always welcome, Chance."

Having the bulk of her dog training at the Boys Ranch had been good. With Chance and Jaris joining the effort, she'd been able to find time to go on her band's out-of-town gigs. God, she loved music almost as much as she loved training her dogs. Her life had really expanded over the past several months for the better.

"Good morning, Miss Kaylyn," the boys said in unison.

"Good morning." Chance held out the cup for her. "This is for you."

"Thank you." She took a sip, glancing up at the six-foot-five hunk of dark chocolate. God, he was so handsome. "Nice and hot." *Just like you.*

Even though Chance was blind, she felt like he could see right through her.

Holding her lips to the rim of the cup, she recalled the one and only kiss she'd shared with Chance at her mother's Christmas party a couple of years ago. That night she'd wanted to talk to Chance about coming to work at her service dog training school. It had been the only thing on her mind and she'd tried to wait for the perfect opportunity to bring up the subject. She did have strong feelings for him, but that night she'd been thinking about the partnership they would form and the amazing work they would be able to do together. She'd hoped that spending more time with Chance would cause him to think of her differently.

Their signals had definitely gotten crossed when someone had mentioned the mistletoe above their heads.

After that toe-curling kiss, Chance had left in a rush, sending a clear message that the most they could ever be was friends.

She'd thought about running after Chance to tell him how much she'd cared for him but hadn't been able to make her feet move. She'd suddenly been paralyzed by doubt and fear. Even though she'd been intent about trying to get him to agree to join her at the dog training school, he'd clearly sensed her unspoken feelings for him that night. He had no interest in her that way.

To this very day they'd never spoken about the kiss again.

Jaris came up with Sugar. He'd been the one who had finally convinced Chance to move to Destiny and work at her school. She was happy but didn't hold on to false hope.

She'd retrieved that sprig of mistletoe the morning after her mother's party and placed it in her nightstand, where it remained to this day, along with the box of condoms she'd bought. Why? She'd held onto the hope that she and Chance would make love that

Christmas. It had turned out nothing like she'd hoped. The mistletoe and condoms were reminders to keep her feelings buried and locked away. Chance was an amazing and wonderful friend. Like it or not, it had to be enough. It would never be more.

"I knew you would be on time, but Chance made me bet against you." The former detective was just as tall as Chance and equally as attractive, though his features were lighter, including his sandy blond hair.

Chance laughed. "You know me better than that, don't you, Kaylyn?"

She smiled. "I think I'll stay out of it, if you don't mind."

Jaris reached into his pocket. "Here you go, Chance." He tossed the coin into the air.

Chance caught it, which never ceased to amaze her. "Best money I made all day."

All the boys' eyes were wide with wonder and one of the older boys asked, "How do you do that, Mr. Chance?"

"That's a great question, Daniel." She turned to Chance. "I'd like to know how you do that, too."

Chance grinned. "It's magic."

She knew it had to do with how attuned his other senses were, but he had never admitted it to her.

Standing by Rosie, little Jake yawned. "Do we get to go with you today, Miss Kaylyn?"

She shook her head. "Not today, Jake. Today is a test day for Rosie and the other dogs."

She would be driving the dogs out to a remote location on the Stone Ranch with Chance and Jaris. Their new owners would be arriving next week for their training and bonding with the new service canines. Rosie and the other dogs needed to be ready to go.

She loved her work but graduation day gave her joy and sadness. As always, after she said good-bye to the dogs and their new owners, the training of the next class of dogs would begin the very next day.

Holding a basket, Belle came out of the main house and walked over. "Good morning."

"Morning." Kaylyn could see the glow in the woman's smile. Not surprising, since Belle was a little over three months pregnant. Soon she would start showing.

"How are the boys doing?" Belle asked.

"They are doing fantastic." Chance moved right next to Kaylyn, causing her temperature to rise a few degrees. "All the dogs were bathed last night and put to bed. The boys got up early this morning to feed them and get the harnesses on. Perfect job."

Belle smiled broadly. "I'm glad to hear that."

"Juan, come over here," Chance said.

"Yes, sir."

Chance placed his hand on Juan's shoulder. "You know you're in charge of Sugar and Annie while we're testing the other dogs. I know I can trust you."

"Yes, sir. I'll take very good care of them." The boy took Sugar and Annie. "Here's Rosie and Rex, Mr. Chance." He handed the leashes over.

"Thanks, Juan."

"And here are King and Blue, Mr. Jaris." Daniel, one of the older boys, gave the leads to him.

"Thanks, buddy."

Juan and Daniel led Sugar and Annie into the house.

Belle turned to the other boys. "Miss Amber has made you all chocolate chip pancakes. Go inside and wash up. I will meet you at the table in five minutes."

The rest of the boys ran into the big house.

Chance placed his arm around Kaylyn's shoulder, causing her heart to skip a couple of beats. "I wouldn't mind some chocolate chip pancakes myself. How about you, Jaris?"

Jaris's lips curled up into a grin making him appear even more handsome. "I could eat. Maybe we should go inside."

Though Kaylyn hated changing her schedule, for them, she would. "Guys, if we need to delay the test we can."

Jaris laughed.

"Just kidding, Kaylyn." Chance released her, and she instantly missed his touch. "We asked Belle to pack us some food for the morning."

Belle handed the basket to Chance. "There is another thermos of coffee for you, as well as some fruit and muffins. When you get back, we'll feed you a proper breakfast."

Jaris loaded up the dogs into the back of the truck.

Shane and Corey ran out of the house, moving quickly to Belle's side.

"Honey, you shouldn't be out here alone." Corey scanned the tree line in the distance with his hand on the butt of his gun.

"I'm not alone. Kaylyn is here and so are Jaris and Chance. I'm perfectly safe."

Kaylyn felt sorry for Belle. Ever since learning that Kip Lunceford wanted her bone marrow, the entire town had become her bodyguard detail. She couldn't go anywhere without an armed escort. It had to be exhausting, but Belle didn't complain.

Corey frowned. "Sweetheart, you know what I mean."

"I do. You and Shane are my overprotective husbands, and I love you for it. I'm sure Chance and Jaris would hear anyone approaching before any of us did. And they have these beautiful dogs that would protect all of us from harm."

Corey turned to Jaris and Chance. "Sorry, guys. Even though we know you are capable, she's our responsibility. You understand?"

"Of course," Chance answered. "If it were Kaylyn, I would feel the same way."

Shocked to hear that, Kaylyn asked, "You would?"

He smiled. "Well, we are best friends, aren't we?"

"I suppose you're right." She sighed as her heart shrank a bit.

Belle turned to her. "Good luck with the test." She and her husbands walked back inside the house.

Kaylyn took a deep breath, steadying herself. "Are you ready to go, guys?"

Jaris walked up to the driver's side door and grabbed her hand, sending a shiver up and down her spine. "Let's get this show on the road, boss."

Over the past few months working with Jaris, she'd found herself imagining what it would be like to be with him and Chance. Why not? She was from Destiny, a place where women were allowed to dream of love with two or more men.

Who couldn't love Jaris? The guy was a hero. Handsome. Charming. And funny. He was so good to the boys and wonderful with the dogs.

Who am I kidding? I'm falling for Jaris, too.

Getting behind the wheel of her truck, she glanced at the men who were invading all her nighttime dreams. As much as she would like to be in their arms, it wasn't going to happen. She had deeper feelings for Chance than he had for her. She'd almost lost him as a friend for good because of those feelings. She vowed not to make the same mistake with Jaris.

Feelings can't be trusted.

* * * *

Chance held Rosie's and Rex's harnesses. He could hear Jaris and the other two dogs up ahead about ten feet on the path. All four dogs were doing great, but he still felt odd being without Annie. If Annie and Sugar had remained close, they would've taken the lead in this test, skewing the results for the new dogs.

Going for help when necessary had to be learned by every service dog. This test would verify these dogs were fully trained to seek aid when their masters were in trouble. He and Jaris had run several exercises with the four and were confident they would pass Kaylyn's standards today.

Kaylyn was two miles back beside her truck.

"The time is 8:29 a.m." *One minute to go until the final part of the test.*

He could hear the waterfall that he and Jaris had passed after leaving Kaylyn. During the entire walk from the truck, the dogs had accomplished their tasks perfectly. They were all completely focused and so far had done exceedingly well on every part of the test. None of the distractions that Kaylyn had planted along the path—raw steak, noisemakers, or toys—had been able to pull Rex, Blue, Rosie, or King from their jobs. He was filled with pride for the four dogs, nearly done with their training and ready to meet their new owners in the next few days.

"The time is 8:30 a.m."

"Now, Jaris." Chance spread out on the ground, hearing his friend do the same.

Rosie and Rex both sniffed and licked him, which was expected. He held his breath and remained motionless.

The two dogs ran off. He heard King and Blue bolt after Rosie and Rex.

Chance waited for a minute before sitting up, making sure the dogs were down the road. It was important not to distract the canine students. They needed to run all the way back to Kaylyn.

Hearing Jaris roll onto his side, Chance turned his direction. "Man, these four are going to make their new owners very happy."

"Just like Annie and Sugar make us happy, buddy." Jaris's tone was filled with admiration.

He smiled. "I hope so. That's why we're working so hard with them."

"It won't be long before Kaylyn will be back with the dogs and the truck to pick us up. I wonder what score she'll give them."

"You know we'll have to give her the results of the preliminary tests during the walk before she comes to a final decision." Kaylyn was one of the top service dog trainers in the country. People from around the world sought out her dogs. "But I'm sure they will all get A-pluses."

Suddenly, he and Jaris heard the four dogs yelp as if they were hurt.

"What the hell was that?" Jaris leapt to his feet.

He did the same. "Don't know, but we've got to get back to Kaylyn."

"Agreed. Let's go."

They started down the path together when they both heard a gunshot.

Chance's gut tightened. "What the fuck?"

Jaris came up beside him. "It sounded like a rifle to me."

They both knew that Kaylyn had a pistol in her truck but not a rifle.

"Shit. We're not alone, Jaris. Someone else is in the woods."

"This is the Stone's property. Private land. We're supposed to be the only fucking ones out here today."

Chance pulled out his cell, running his fingers over the numbers in Braille. He dialed Kaylyn's phone. It rang once and then her voice mail came on. "Fuck, Jaris. Kaylyn isn't picking up. It went straight to voice mail."

"I'm calling the Stones."

He dialed Kaylyn again. Same result. "God, please let her be okay."

"Emmett's phone is ringing, buddy."

That was a good thing since reception was spotty on the ranch. Maybe that was the reason he'd gotten Kaylyn's voice mail so quickly. She might've been in a dead spot.

"Hey, Emmett. This is Jaris. We heard a fucking rifle fire out here. We can't get ahold of Kaylyn and the dogs are gone." Jaris paused.

"So nobody should be out here? That's what we thought. We're out on the sunrise road. She parked about a mile before the waterfall. We're about two miles up the road from her and we're headed her direction now." Hearing Jaris pause again, Chance felt every tick of the clock. "Fuck. Please hurry, Emmett." Jaris clicked off his phone. "Chance, Emmett's on his way but he is in town with the boys and his brothers. It'll take too much time before he can reach Kaylyn."

"We've got to get to her, Jaris." His heart pounded hard in his chest.

"Agreed."

As they headed down the path, Chance thought about shouting commands for the dogs to return, but decided against it. Until they knew who had fired the rifle, it was best to keep quiet.

Kip Lunceford had leukemia and wanted Belle's bone marrow. The killer was still on the loose, and Belle lived on this ranch. Like it or not, there was a distinct possibility that the gunshot they'd heard had come from that bastard or one of his cohorts. He and Jaris had no other choice but to try to reach Kaylyn, regardless how difficult it would be without Annie and Sugar.

"If the dogs made it back to Kaylyn, she'll be headed this way." Jaris was clearly running through a myriad of possibilities, hoping she was safe.

"That's true." But after hearing the yelping, his gut told him they hadn't.

Several minutes passed in silence. No dogs. No Kaylyn.

"Did you hear that?" Jaris asked, suddenly stopping on the path.

He listened intently, focusing all his attention on the sounds around him. "That's a truck, but it doesn't sound like Kaylyn's."

"I know."

"Wait, Jaris. That's two trucks."

"I hear them, too."

It sounded like the vehicles drove off in opposite directions.

They hastened their steps to Kaylyn.

When they got next to the waterfall, he heard Jaris stumble.

"Fuck."

"You okay, Jaris?"

"Fine. Just a dip in the fucking road."

Chance's pulse shot hot through his veins. They had to work together to get to Kaylyn. "Let's lock arms. It'll help stabilize us."

"Good idea, buddy. Don't forget the path curves to the right up ahead."

"I remember." Being without Annie was proving more difficult than he'd imagined, but it didn't matter. He had to get to Kaylyn and make sure she was okay.

Suddenly, they heard honking.

"That's Kaylyn's truck," Jaris said.

"I recognize it, too."

They picked up their pace, heading toward the sound.

"Kaylyn has got to be okay, Chance."

"I hope so, but I keep asking myself why she wouldn't have come to us."

"Maybe one of the dogs is hurt and she can't leave them yet." Was Jaris grasping at straws, trying to calm his worry for Kaylyn? Yes.

God, I hope he's right and she's okay.

They continued down the path for what felt like an eternity. Finally, he and Jaris rounded the last corner where they'd left Kaylyn earlier.

"Over here, guys." Her voice sounded sweeter than anything he'd ever heard before in his life. "Just a few more feet. Where are the dogs?"

"We don't know," Jaris said. "We thought they were with you. We heard a rifle shot."

"You heard that?" Kaylyn's tone didn't sit well with him.

He reached out and touched her face. Sensing she was holding something back, his gut coiled into a knot of concern. "Kaylyn, are you okay?"

"I'm okay, Chance."

He felt a tear on her cheek and stiffened. "What's the matter?"

"Don't worry. I really am okay, but I have been shot."

Chapter Three

"Where are you shot?" As Jaris knelt down in front of Kaylyn, he could smell the faint aroma of metal, which was a sure sign she was bleeding.

"I promise you I'm okay."

"I'll be the judge of that." His experience on the force in Chicago kicked in. Blind or not, he needed to fully assess the situation. "Tell me where you are shot, Kaylyn."

"In my right leg. Chance, there's a first aid kit in my glove box."

He could hear Chance walk over to the passenger door.

Jaris ran his hand gently up Kaylyn's leg and felt her thigh bleeding. "It's a good thing you wore shorts today."

"It was such a beautiful morning, how could I not? I had no idea this was going to happen."

"None of us did." From what he could tell, she was right that it wasn't life threatening, but they did need to get the bleeding stopped. "Did you see the shooter?"

"No, but I think whoever shot me was somewhere to the north of us, up the rise."

Chance returned with the kit. In a flash they had her wound cleaned and bandaged.

"I'm going to see if I can get a signal to call Doc." Chance would've made one helluva good cop. He definitely had the heart and mind for it even if he didn't have the eyes.

"I've tried to call out but haven't been able to." Kaylyn sounded so brave.

"Sweetheart, I'll walk a few steps away," Chance said. "You know how the reception is out here. A few feet can make all the difference."

Jaris listened to his friend move off to the left.

"Can you stand, Kaylyn?" He wanted to get her into the cab, since it offered a little bit of cover, though definitely not enough.

"I think so."

He knew that the shooter might still be close.

"Emmett, this is Chance. Kaylyn's been shot."

"Jaris, I can't believe he got a signal."

Thank God, he got through.

As Chance continued telling Emmett about what was going on, Jaris ran through all the things they knew so far in his mind. It was obvious that whoever shot her wasn't in the trucks that he and Chance had heard earlier. Those vehicles had been near the waterfall. The gunshot had happened before they had driven off. There didn't seem to be a connection, but his days on the Chicago PD told him there might be.

Chance returned. "Emmett was already on his way. He's going to call Doc to head up here, too. Cody and Bryant are with the boys in town."

"Excellent. Let's get her into the truck."

They helped Kaylyn to her feet, placing her in the backseat with her head in Chance's lap and her feet in his, allowing her to elevate her wounded leg.

They shut the doors, listening to every sound outside the vehicle. So far, there was no indication that the shooter was still around.

"Did you see any trucks, Kaylyn?" Chance asked.

"No. I haven't seen anything or anyone. I'm so worried about the dogs, guys." Her voice shook. "I heard them yelping and they haven't come back. We need to go looking for them."

"No," Jaris stated firmly. "Too big a risk. Someone shot you. They might still be out there."

"I'm betting it was a hunter." Hearing her voice shake just a little revealed to him she wasn't so sure.

He thought about telling her what Emmett had told him earlier—that no one should be out this way—but decided against it. No need in worrying her more.

"That might be true but clearly whoever it was is reckless." He grabbed her hand and squeezed. "We need to get back to the ranch house so that we aren't sitting ducks."

"And Kaylyn needs medical attention." Chance sighed. "Walking is out of the question with the injury to her leg. Maybe we could try to carry her."

"No." He knew what they had to do. "I'm driving."

"You're what?" Kaylyn's doubt was obvious in her tone.

"Are you serious, buddy?" Chance didn't seem sure his idea would work, although he clearly agreed they should get out of there fast.

"Very."

"Emmett is headed our way." Chance had a point, but Jaris knew in these kinds of situations, seconds mattered. Who knew when Emmett would show? "Shouldn't we wait for him?"

"No. We can do this, buddy." He grabbed Kaylyn's hand and squeezed. "It's going to be okay."

She squeezed back. "Jaris, you haven't forgotten you are blind, have you?"

"Of course not, but I drove for years before I got shot."

Kaylyn touched his jaw with her fingers. "But you cannot see now. We should wait for Emmett. He'll be here soon. I still think this was a freak accident and has nothing to do with Lunceford."

Hearing the bastard's name made him want to protect her all the more. *Sight or no sight, I'm going to get that psycho.*

He moved his hand down Kaylyn's leg. "The bleeding seems to have stopped. Let's get her in the front seat. She will be my eyes."

Kaylyn removed her fingers from his face. "Are you sure about this? We could just stay low in the truck until the Stones get here."

He could tell she was more nervous about the shooter than she was letting on.

"Absolutely." Her protection was all that mattered to him now.

Quickly, they helped her into the passenger's side and Chance returned to the back of the cab.

He jumped into the driver's seat, placing his hands on the steering wheel. "Kaylyn, do you have the keys?"

"They're still in the ignition."

Though it had been a long time since he'd been in this position in any vehicle, it felt familiar. Keeping his left hand on the wheel, he touched the key with his right hand. *Like riding a bike—but driving a car? Either way, you never forget.*

He turned the key, and the truck's engine roared to life. "Okay, Kaylyn. You ready?"

"Yes, but let's go slow. Deal?"

"Sure."

Thankfully, Kaylyn's truck had automatic transmission. It would make this trip easier, though in his sighted days he'd always preferred manual transmission.

He put his foot on the brake and moved the gearshift down to what he felt was "drive." "This is the right gear, Kaylyn?"

"Perfect. You certainly still have the feel for driving."

"Okay, we've got to get turned around. Is there enough room here to do that?"

"Yes. We're parked on the side off of the road, so you've got room to do a U-turn. You'll need to cut it sharp because there's a slight drop-off on the other side of the road."

"Got it." He moved his foot off the brake and to the gas pedal. He applied a little pressure to the accelerator and turned the wheel hard to the left.

"That's perfect, Jaris." Kaylyn's tone was shaky, which told him she was nervous about this.

He wasn't. With her as his guide he was confident they could drive all the way to California and back if necessary.

He straightened out the wheel, realizing they'd made the full turn. "Am I on the road now, Kaylyn?"

"A little to the right and you'll be lined up perfectly. You got it. This is so crazy." Kaylyn laughed.

"What's so funny, sweetheart?" Chance asked, also laughing. "A blind chauffeur is all the rage these days, haven't you heard?"

"Maybe so, but I think once my leg is fixed up, we'll leave the driving to me. Jaris, there's a curve up ahead to the right."

"Sharp or slight?"

"Slight. Start moving right...now. Perfect. Straighten it out. Excellent."

"How fast am I going?"

"Ten miles an hour."

"Let's kick it up a little." He wanted to get clear of the danger and closer to where she could have her leg looked at by the doctor.

"Okay. This is a pretty straight shot for a few miles."

"Tell me when we're up to twenty."

They continued down the ranch road with Kaylyn giving directions and him driving for several minutes. It felt good to be behind the wheel again, even without his eyes. It felt normal.

"There's a truck headed our direction, guys."

"I recognize that engine," Chance said. "That's Emmett's truck."

Jaris knew Chance was right, hearing the familiar sound of the engine up ahead. He removed his foot from the gas pedal and over to the brake, bringing the vehicle to a stop. "You're right. It is Emmett's truck," Kaylyn said. "Lyle is in the passenger seat."

Jaris stiffened when he heard a second engine, following behind. "Do you recognize the other vehicle, Chance?" He reached into his pocket for his gun.

"Nope." His friend's tone told him that he was wondering if the vehicle trailing Emmett could be one of the two trucks they'd heard earlier, too.

And what about the shooter? The creep likely had driven onto the ranch as well.

Things weren't adding up.

He was prepared to take off again if necessary. Kaylyn was his priority.

Kaylyn sighed. "I can't believe this."

Jaris gripped the steering wheel with one hand and the handle of his pistol with the other. "Believe what?"

"It's the ambulance, guys. Relax."

He let out a big breath of relief, letting go of his gun. "Good for Doc. That is excellent thinking."

"But I don't need an ambulance."

"Let's let Doc be the judge of that, sweetheart," Chance said from the backseat. "He's the one who's been to medical school."

"Chance is right, Kaylyn. I'm sure Doc just wanted to have all the equipment he might need. After all, he doesn't know how bad your wound is."

"Maybe so, but I still think the ambulance is overkill."

He heard the two vehicles come to a stop next to them.

"Good grief," Kaylyn said. "Mick, Doc's brother, is driving the ambulance and Paris is sitting between him and Doc. They must think I'm dying. Here they all come running."

Chance got out of the cab of the truck, but Jaris stayed put, though he opened his door. Doc and Paris immediately went to work on Kaylyn, keeping her in her seat for the moment.

"Miss Anderson, are you okay?" Lyle was obviously shaken. The guy clearly looked up to Kaylyn like she was his sister.

"I'm fine, Lyle. Did the dogs show back up at the ranch?"

"No."

Jaris found that odd.

"Good God, Jaris," Emmett said. "Were you driving?"

He nodded. "And damn good, too. I think I'm ready for NASCAR."

Emmett, Mick, and Chance laughed, but all of their attention was really on what was going on in the passenger seat of Kaylyn's truck. Was she okay? Until he heard Doc's final assessment, he wouldn't relax.

As the medical duo checked Kaylyn's vitals, Emmett and Mick, in low tones, asked questions about the shooting. He and Chance told them about the two trucks they'd heard and about the missing dogs.

"I contacted Jason right after I got your call." Emmett was one of those guys who kept his head under any kind of pressure. Good thing. The sheriff needed to investigate what went down up here. If they were lucky, Jason would apprehend the shooter before the bastard could get away. "He and Nicole should be here any minute. Mick, why don't you and I check the perimeter in case the shooter followed them?"

"You bet," Doc's brother said.

One thing about Destiny, everyone stuck together when things got tough, and with Lunceford still on the loose, things had been really tough for everyone.

Jaris leaned in closer to Kaylyn, listening to Doc and Paris take care of her. "Doc, how is she?"

"Doing great. You and Chance did a fantastic job bandaging her wound. Very impressive."

"It looks to be just a flesh wound, Jaris," Paris informed. "She's going to be fine."

"I agree," Doc said. "I still want to put her in the ambulance and get her back to the clinic. A few stitches and some antibiotics is all she'll need. After that, I'm sure she'll be as good as new."

"Ambulance?" Kaylyn obviously wasn't keen on that idea. "Doc, I don't need to ride to town in an ambulance."

"The bleeding has stopped but we don't want to aggravate it and get it started again, Kaylyn." Doc was a no-nonsense kind of guy, which he admired.

Jaris placed his hand on Kaylyn's shoulder. *She's safe. Thank God.* "Sweetheart, do as Doc says."

Chapter Four

Jaris just called me "sweetheart." That's a first. Kaylyn looked at him still seated behind the wheel of her truck. "No sense in arguing with you, is there?"

"None," the former cop said.

"Chance, are you on his side on this?" How many times had she heard Chance call her "sweetheart"? Almost every day, but the word to him clearly only meant friendship.

"You bet I am."

She smiled. "Since I'm so outnumbered, I guess I don't have a choice."

They all helped her into the back of the ambulance and onto the stretcher.

"Lyle and I will stay put until the sheriff arrives," Emmett said. "We'll find the guy who shot you, Kaylyn."

"Would you call to check to see if the four dogs returned to the ranch house, please?"

"I already did." He frowned. "I'm sorry, but there's been no sign of them."

"That doesn't make any sense." Her eyes welled up with tears. "Those dogs are highly trained. Even if something got them off track and they couldn't make it back to the truck they should've gone back to the ranch house."

"Amber will call me if they show up. Don't forget, those dogs are all chipped. If they somehow make it to another county or town, someone will scan them I'm sure. We'll have them back soon. Shane and Corey are with her and Belle making sure everything is okay."

"We better get going," Paris said.

She and Doc remained with her in the back, and Jaris and Chance went up to the front with Mick, who was going to drive the ambulance.

As the vehicle began to move down the road, her mind started spinning.

Please, God, let the dogs be okay.

Where could they be? What happened to them? What was she going to do if they couldn't be found? There were four people who would be arriving in Destiny soon who needed Rex, Blue, King, and Rosie.

I just can't figure this out.

Doc continued examining her wound while Paris placed a blood pressure cuff on her left arm.

I can't believe I've been shot. Did this have anything to do with Kip Lunceford? Obviously it was something all of them were considering. But it didn't make any sense. The psycho wanted Belle, not her. *Why would he shoot me? Or have me shot?*

Chance and Jaris had been amazing through all of it, making sure she was okay and safe. She still couldn't believe they'd made it all the way back to her truck on foot without the dogs. The ranch road wasn't an easy walk for anyone, let alone guys who were blind.

Chance never ceased to surprise her. He could do absolutely anything. Anyone looking on would've thought he had his sight. He'd acted quickly and without hesitation, checking to make sure she was okay, getting the first aid kit, dressing her wound, and so much more.

The only thing he seems to be blind about is my feelings for him.

Jaris had driven so well it had shocked her. Unlike Chance, who had been born blind, Jaris had lost his sight after being shot trying to save Nicole, his former partner. Before he'd come to work for her, she'd talked with Nicole about him. Nicole had told her that his doctors had said due to the type of injury he'd sustained, there was a very slim chance Jaris's sight would return someday. Since learning that, Kaylyn had prayed every night it would.

They were great men and her heroes. Without them she would've been in real trouble today.

"120 over 72," Paris told Doc.

"Perfect." Doc smiled down at her. "We'll be in town shortly, Kaylyn. You're doing great."

"Thanks to you and Paris."

"And to Chance and Jaris, too." Paris winked. "They're the heroes of the day."

"That's for sure." Kaylyn's mind kept replaying Jaris calling her sweetheart. She wondered what he meant by it. Was it only the moment or something more? In her heart she wished it were the "something more."

Damn, Kaylyn. Don't make more out of it than what it is.

She'd misread signals once before and almost lost Chance for good.

I will not make that mistake again.

* * * *

At the clinic, Chance held Kaylyn's hand. Jaris stood on the other side of the bed, holding her other hand.

"I wish Doc would hurry up and release me."

"You need to be patient, sweetheart." Chance gently squeezed her fingers. He'd almost lost her today.

God, what would I have done without her?

"There's only one wing of the clinic completed, guys."

"We both know that, sweetheart." Chance realized she was trying to make an argument to be sprung early, but she was right. Lucas Wolfe and team had put a rush on the construction. There was more left to complete the entire project, but with this portion of the building done it gave the citizens of Destiny a modern high-tech place that they needed for their sick and injured.

"There really are only three rooms finished. Someone like me doesn't need to be taking up a bed. I'm fine." She never had liked being on the receiving end of help, always preferring to be the one who *helped* others instead.

Even though he loved Kaylyn's sassiness, he wasn't about to let her walk out of here without the all clear from Doc. He'd never been so worried about anyone in all his life. He took a deep breath, reminding himself she was okay and he would make damn sure she would stay that way.

"You need to just settle down and lean back on your pillow," he told her firmly. "You're not going anywhere. Besides, the other two rooms are empty. You're Doc's only patient at the moment, so you're not taking anyone else's room."

The door opened.

"Hi, guys." The voice was from the deputy sheriff, Nicole Coleman, former partner of Jaris. "How are you doing, Kaylyn?"

"I'm fine," she answered. "Have you heard from the sheriff? Have they found my dogs?"

"No sign of them yet. I just talked to Jason. They found a gun casing just north of where Kaylyn's truck was parked. They also found some tire tracks from two trucks."

"What about the shooter?" Jaris asked.

"No news yet on that, but the team is still out on the ranch looking for clues. Jason said the bullet was a .30-06 Springfield cartridge."

"That's a big caliber for this time of year. I thought deer and elk season didn't start in Colorado until fall," Jaris said.

"That's true." Nicole's tone was a little deeper than Kaylyn's, yet still very feminine. "Even most small game licenses don't start until later. Except for some of the year-around game like doves and grouse, hunting is off-limits now. Jason has put in a call to Brock Powers."

"Who is he?" Chance asked.

Kaylyn answered, "He's the game warden in this area. You and Jaris met his brother Blaine. Blaine's the one who brought the horses so we could test how the dogs would react."

"The rancher," he said. "I remember him."

Nicole continued, "The tracks Jason and the others found came together by Sycamore Pond. Seems like the men who were trespassing on Stone Ranch met up there."

"Do you think this could be connected to Lunceford somehow?" Kaylyn asked.

Chance's gut tightened. He wasn't about to let anyone, let alone Destiny's worst enemy, harm her.

"Maybe," the deputy said. "We know for sure that Lunceford wants Belle, but we can't figure out why he would shoot Kaylyn. We can't find the connection."

"The bastard has declared war on the whole town." Jaris's tone held an edge of rage. "We all know he would love nothing more than to burn Destiny and all its people to ashes."

Chance knew he could count on his friend to help protect Kaylyn. "That creep is a complete psychopath. No one is safe until he's dead and buried."

"Or behind bars," Nicole said.

"Nicole, don't give the law enforcement line." Jaris was as frustrated about what Lunceford had done to Destiny as anyone. "We all know prison was never able to hold him."

The deputy sighed. "True. We actually don't have a lot to go on now, but I'm sure we will find whoever is responsible for shooting Kaylyn."

"Nicole, please call Jason and make sure he keeps looking for my dogs." The fear in Kaylyn's voice crushed him.

Chance understood her worry. Not having Annie by his side didn't sit right with him but it was unavoidable. Naturally they had come straight to the clinic.

"We will keep looking for them. I promise." Nicole was a fantastic person and law enforcement officer. She cared deeply about her job and about the people of Destiny.

Kaylyn's cell rang. "Oh boy. It's my mother. Hi, Mom. I'm fine."

Her mother had gone with her cousin to Hawaii two days ago for a two-week vacation, something she'd always wanted to do.

"Don't you dare cut your trip short, Mom. I'm fine. I swear. Yes, he is. Chance, she wants to talk to you." Kaylyn's voice lowered. "You better back me up, mister."

"Sure, sweetheart."

Kaylyn handed him the phone.

"Hi, Betty."

"Chance, tell me the truth. Kaylyn is okay?" The woman's voice shook.

"She's fine." The door opened and he heard the footsteps he knew came from Doc. "The doctor is here now. Would you like to talk to him?"

"Dammit, Chance. Give me the phone back."

He grinned, knowing he'd pulled a fast one on Kaylyn.

"Yes," Kaylyn's mother said. "Please let me talk to Dr. Ryder."

"Doc, I have Betty on the phone. She wants to know that her little girl is okay."

Doc took the cell. "Hi, Mrs. Anderson. Kaylyn is going to be fine. It was only a flesh wound but deep enough that I want her to stay off her legs for a few days. Paris is bringing in a wheelchair and some crutches for her to take home with her. Yes, ma'am. I will. I promise. Chance she wants to talk to you again."

"I think you are all going overboard about this. I'm fine." Kaylyn's frustration was clear. "I need to get back to work. I need to find my dogs."

Ignoring her, he took the cell from Doc. "Hi again."

"Do you think I should come back, Chance?"

"No. Kaylyn is fine."

"I believe you, but you need to promise me something."

"Of course."

"Make sure Kaylyn does what the doctor says, Chance."

"Jaris and I will make sure she follows his orders. I swear. Nothing is going to happen to her."

"Promise me you'll call me if I'm needed for any reason."

"I promise, but don't you worry. You've wanted this trip for as far back as I can remember. So please just enjoy yourself. It would make Kaylyn very upset if she did anything to ruin your vacation."

"Thank you, Chance," Kaylyn whispered.

"I trust you, young man," her mother said. "But I will be calling every day."

"And we will be looking forward to hearing from you, Betty."

"I'd like to talk to my daughter again, if you don't mind."

He handed the phone back to Kaylyn.

"Hi, Mom."

The door opened again.

"Here's Kaylyn's ride," Paris said.

"A wheelchair? Oh brother. Yes, Mom. I promise to do what Doc, Chance, and Jaris say."

As Kaylyn and her mother continued talking, he vowed silently to himself to not only make sure Kaylyn followed every one of Doc's orders but also to make sure she remained safe.

Chapter Five

Being rolled out of the clinic in a wheelchair didn't sit right with Kaylyn, but what choice did she have? Everyone was bent on her staying off that leg. This whole thing was being blown out of proportion. Chance and Jaris were the worst offenders, though in truth she liked the attention she was receiving from the gorgeous men.

Each of them held on to one of the handles of her wheelchair, while Mick directed them to Paris's car. She was so thankful for Jaris and Chance's help.

She knew they wanted and needed Sugar and Annie back by their sides. Thankfully, Emmett had called to say he was bringing their dogs from the ranch and would meet them at her house.

Paris was up ahead by her car, opening all the doors.

"Guys, move her a little to the left," Mick told them. "Perfect. Ten more feet and we're there."

"Thanks, Paris, for being such a good friend." Kaylyn cared deeply for her. The two of them had gotten really close. "I appreciate you driving us to my house."

"No problem, Kaylyn." Paris turned to Mick. "Let's put our patient in the backseat."

"Jaris and I will help her into your car." Chance locked the brakes of the chair.

She loved how caring he and Jaris were being with her.

"Hold on, buddy. Let me get in first so I can help get her settled." Jaris placed his hands on the car, moving to the other side of the vehicle. He entered the backseat and slid over. "Ready, Chance?"

"Ready." Chance lifted her off the wheelchair and into his muscled chest, taking her breath away for a moment. "You okay, Kaylyn?"

"I'm fine." *More than fine.*

Chance stepped forward and lowered her down into Jaris's arms.

"Guys, I can slide over to the middle on my own."

"Maybe so, but we're not going to let you put pressure on your leg. You seem to forget how deep your flesh wound is, Kaylyn." Jaris slid over, keeping hold of her until she was in the very center of the backseat.

Chance sat down on the other side of her and pulled the door closed.

"Everyone buckled up?" Paris started the car.

Mick turned around from the passenger's seat and inspected all of them. "All set. We're ready to roll."

Chance and Jaris both grabbed one of her hands. Did their feelings for her go beyond just friendship? *Am I just fooling myself once again?* She didn't have a clue.

Mick put his arm around Paris's shoulder and Kaylyn saw her shiver.

It was clear to her that Paris wanted the same kind of attention with Doc and Mick that she was currently enjoying from Chance and Jaris. The two brothers treated Paris more like a good friend most of the time, but Kaylyn knew better. She'd caught Doc and Mick, when they thought no one was looking, gazing at Paris in ways that made it obvious they saw her as more than just a friend. They saw her as a woman. How long before those three figured out they were meant for each other?

Why am I able to see clearly what those around me feel about each other but I can't figure out what Chance and Jaris really feel for me?

* * * *

Jaris had been to Kaylyn and her mother's house many times, helping them make dinner, which made things easier for him.

Three steps to the refrigerator. Two steps left to the stove. Turn around and one step to the sink.

He opened the cabinet to the left of the oven and pulled out a spice bottle. He took off the cap and sniffed. Celery salt. *That's not what I need for my spaghetti sauce.* After a couple of attempts he found the garlic and other spices he wanted.

"Sugar, you think Kaylyn will want red or white wine?"

He heard his sweet companion bark, remaining on the floor by his feet.

He laughed. "I agree, girl. Red will be perfect."

Kaylyn kept her whites in the refrigerator and her reds in the cabinet. He pulled out a red and opened it to let it breathe. He got three wine glasses out and set them by the bottle.

"Damn it. Kaylyn can't have wine. She's on medication." He thought about putting the cork back into the bottle, but decided not to. Chance could have some and so could he. "Guess she'll have to settle for soda, Sugar."

Chance was with Kaylyn in her bedroom, where they'd gotten her settled after Paris and Mick dropped them off.

Stirring the sauce, his mind drifted back to earlier this morning. Kaylyn had been shot. He could've lost her.

His fingers tightened on the spoon. "Sugar, what would we do without her? Thank God, we don't have to know."

The shooter was still on the loose. He and Chance weren't going to leave Kaylyn's side until the fucker was found.

Keeping Kaylyn off her feet was going to be difficult because she wanted to start in the morning looking for the missing dogs. No way were he and Chance going to let her out until Doc released her to walk.

"Kaylyn is amazing, isn't she, Sugar?" Talking to his dog was easy for him. He could trust Sugar with his life, and he knew not to trust anyone who didn't like animals. "Kaylyn is the perfect woman in every way. She is loyal to her friends, her family, and even to precious dogs like you. Sugar, don't you think Kaylyn will make a wonderful mother someday?" *Unlike my own mother.*

He heard Chance and Annie heading toward the kitchen.

"Whatever you're cooking sure smells good."

"Spaghetti. How's our patient, buddy?"

Chance laughed. "Not so patient, if you know what I mean. When she hears you're preparing spaghetti, she's going to want to eat in the dining room instead of the bedroom."

"Damn, I hadn't thought of that. She is a neat freak, isn't she?"

"She sure is," Chance said.

"She's not going to have any choice. You and I both know she can't be on that leg too much."

"I agree."

"Here's a bottle of red, a soda, and two glasses for both of you."

"Wine for me and soda for her because of her medications, right?"

"Right."

Chance took the beverages. "What about you, Jaris? What are you drinking?"

"I'll bring my own glass and share the wine with you after I'm finished. I'll have this ready in about five minutes. Go try to soften her up about the meal. Tell her that I'll make sure it's all cleaned up afterward. There won't be a crumb left behind."

"You got a deal." Chance took Annie back to Kaylyn's bedroom.

Jaris tasted the sauce, and then added a bit more garlic. As he stirred the pot, he thought about how gone Chance was for Kaylyn. They'd known each other for years. He had a pretty good idea that Kaylyn had feelings for Chance, too. They belonged together. Not him. He was the new man in her life. She and Chance had history, and it was time for them to move forward. Just a little push was all that was needed, and he was ready to make that happen tonight.

He took another taste of the sauce. "Just right, Sugar."

Relationships required the right kind of ingredients to work, just like his sauce. As much as he loved imagining himself with Kaylyn, he knew she and Chance would make the perfect couple.

He reached down and patted Sugar on the head. "You're my girl, aren't you?"

She rubbed against his leg.

The words of his father swirled in his mind. "We Simmons men don't have good luck with women, son."

As he plated up the three dishes for Kaylyn, Chance, and him, Jaris mentally buried his feelings for her down deep in his core. It was for the best.

* * * *

Kaylyn leaned back on the pile of pillows Chance and Jaris had placed on her bed. Besides the two fluffy ones she already had, the guys had pulled out four more from the hall closet. Their bedside manner was to the extreme, though she still enjoyed all the attention.

Chance walked back into the bedroom with Annie. He was carrying several items tucked under his arm. "Dinner should be here any second. We thought it would be fun to eat in your room."

Fun? I know better. They didn't want her to walk to the dining room.

"This should keep your bed clean." Chance spread a tablecloth out over her bedspread.

She laughed, seeing he'd brought out one with Christmas images on it.

"What's so funny, Kaylyn?"

"The tablecloth has Santa and reindeer on it. Wrong time of year."

"Is it?" He laughed. "I think we should sing Christmas carols until Jaris comes in with our food."

"I would but I need to save my voice for the band. We perform for the opening ceremony of Dragon Week tomorrow night."

"Come on, Kaylyn." Chance hummed a few bars of her favorite Christmas song, and then began singing aloud, "…had a very shiny nose. Join me."

"You're a mess, Chance Reynolds." She loved his humor. Always had. Actually, she loved everything about him. *Always had.* "And if you ever saw it—"

"Christmas carols in March?" Jaris came in with Sugar, carrying their dinner.

She and Chance burst into laughter. When she was finally able to compose herself, she explained to Jaris about the tablecloth.

He grinned.

God, I can't get over his grin. "Smells delicious, Jaris. I love your spaghetti."

"I remember you did. I also made us some garlic bread to go with it."

They ate the meal together, humming other carols between bites. After they finished, Jaris and Chance gathered up the dishes and placed the tray by the door.

"My mom taught me not to sing during dinner but this is so much fun."

"We promise not to tell. Besides, I love hearing you sing. You have the most beautiful voice I've ever heard." Jaris shook his head. "I'm getting off track."

"Off track from what?" she asked.

"Nothing. Sorry. We just all have a lot on our minds. I would like to know how you two met." Jaris's sudden subject change seemed odd to her. He folded his arms over his chest. "Details. When? Where? That kind of thing."

She looked over at Chance. "I'm not sure where to begin. Are you?"

"Not really. It's seems like we've always known each other."

Jaris laughed. "Okay. I didn't want to do this but it looks like I must."

"Do what?"

"I was one of Chicago PD's best interrogators. I know how to get people talking, and clearly you two need my expertise. How old were you when you met Chance?"

"I'd just turned nineteen." She closed her eyes and the memory of that day appeared in her mind. "Chance was twenty-two."

"That's right." Chance grabbed her hand and squeezed it, sending a spark up her arm and into her heart. "I was still grieving the loss of my first companion and friend, Sarge."

Jaris sighed. "I didn't know you ever had another service dog besides Annie."

"I did. I got Sarge when I was seven. I had him for fifteen years. I knew I needed another dog and did a search on the web. That's how I discovered Kaylyn."

"The weird thing is, Jaris, though mom and I had been raising service dogs for some time, I'd only put up our website the very day Chance contacted me. What are the odds?"

"Sounds like fate to me, Kaylyn. You two were destined to meet each other." Something in Jaris's tone didn't sit right with her, but she couldn't figure out what. "So you trained Annie?"

"I did. She was one of my best."

"You know the drill, Jaris. Kaylyn requires new owners to stay an entire week before she releases the dogs to them."

"Back then, I only trained one dog at a time, unlike now."

"So you and Chance were alone during that week?"

It seemed like Jaris wanted this conversation to go a certain direction, and that was suddenly making her uncomfortable. "We're friends. Good friends. That's all."

"Really? I think it's deeper than that with both of you."

Was he playing matchmaker? Why? She'd been down that road before and her heart had been broken. "Let's change the subject."

Jaris leaned forward. "No, Kaylyn. We almost lost you today. You and Chance shouldn't be willing to let things that need to be said go unspoken anymore. I've been around you two for some time. I know what is really going on. I know how you feel about each other even if you haven't been able to say it aloud."

She felt tears well up in her eyes. The truth was too painful. "Jaris, please. I know this has been a terrible day for all of us, but—"

"Hold on, Kaylyn. Chance, are you willing to keep silent about how you really feel about her? After today, I can't imagine you would. You're my friend and I know you're not a fool. You have a beautiful woman here that means so much to you. Tell her how you really feel."

"Jaris, you're wrong." Chance's words destroyed her.

She closed her eyes and the tears ran down her cheeks.

"Wrong about what?" Jaris asked.

"Wrong about me not being a fool. I have been a fool. I've been one for a very long time. No more." Chance squeezed her fingers and brought his hand up to her face. "Kaylyn, do you remember that time we kissed under the mistletoe?"

She swallowed hard. "Yes. I will never forget."

"Neither will I. I don't want to lose you, but I can't hold back how I feel about you any longer. You are my friend, my best friend, but damn it, I want more. I've always wanted more. I haven't told you because I realized that night at the Christmas party that you didn't think of me as anything but a friend."

She was shocked by his words. "What? But I thought—"

He placed his fingers to her lips. "Please let me finish before you say anything. I've kept silent all these years, fearing I would lose you. Being close to you, even if it was just as friends, has been the best thing in my life. You make me happy every day." He ran his fingers over her face, seeing her with his touch. "You're beautiful. You're smart. Kind. Generous. And so much more. I don't deserve you, but I do want you. I love you, Kaylyn. Even if you don't feel the same about me, I had to let you know. Jaris was right about that. I couldn't let it go unsaid a second longer."

She wrapped her arms around Chance. "I love you, too. I always have."

"You love me? Really love me?"

"Yes. I love you with all my heart."

He pulled her in closer, pressing his lips to hers. She melted into him, as the years of longing were finally over.

"Chance, your words could've been mine. I thought you didn't have the same feelings for me that I had for you." She kissed him again, feeling so happy. "Jaris made this possible for us. He saw through our walls and got us to open up."

"Yes, he did."

"My work here is done." Jaris sighed. "I think it's time for me to make myself scarce. I'll stay in the guest bedroom, if you don't mind. Good night."

"Jaris, wait. I…want…"

He turned back.

"I just want to thank you for this." *Why am I holding back again?*

He nodded, and before she could say a word, he left with Sugar.

Should she have confessed her feelings for him, too? Being so open and filled with joy, it would've been so easy.

Her mind spun with questions, but when Chance kissed her again, everything seemed to quiet, sending her into a place of utter bliss.

"I can't believe this is happening," she confessed.

He ran his fingers through her hair. "Me either, but I'm so happy it is, Kaylyn. I love you so much. Knowing you feel the same about me has made me the happiest man in the world. I can't wait to make love to you."

She giggled. "Not before Doc releases me, right?"

He smiled. "Right."

"We've waited this long. I guess we can wait a little longer. But first thing in the morning we're going to Doc's office. He'll give me a release or I swear I'll punch him in the face."

He laughed. "That's one of the things I love about you, Kaylyn. You're feisty."

"Once I get back on my feet, you're going to really find out how feisty I can be, Mr. Reynolds." She leaned her head into his muscled chest.

"If I have anything to do with it, you won't be on your feet, baby." He kissed her again, and she felt her heart swell.

Her dream had come true. Chance was holding her, kissing her, confessing his love to her.

Chapter Six

Jaris clicked the remote, flipping through several channels, trying to keep his mind occupied. Even though he couldn't see the television in the guest bedroom, he thought the noise would help lull him to sleep.

It hadn't worked. Neither had the bottle of wine he'd brought with him from the kitchen. He'd drunk the last drop over an hour ago, and still all he could think about was Kaylyn.

He wanted her to be happy. He wanted Chance to be happy. They belonged together. He knew it deep down in his heart, but that didn't make it any easier for him.

Leaning over the side of the bed, he rubbed Sugar on the head. "You're the only one for me, girl."

His eyes were open, but—like all his days and nights had been for over a year—there was only blackness.

Some would look at his life and think it had all been blackness, but they'd be wrong.

Sure, his mother had abandoned him when he was seven and it had been hard, but his dad had remained.

Dad. The man was his hero to this very day. Like Jaris, his dad had been a cop with the Chicago PD. They'd actually been on the force for a couple of years together, though Jaris had been a green rookie and his dad a seasoned cop.

Jaris had been on patrol across town when he'd learned about his dad's heroism and death on the police radio. His father's partner had been hit and was on the ground. They'd come upon a shootout between rival gangs. His dad had covered his partner with his own body, and ended up taking several shots. His father's partner had survived, though his dad had not.

Losing his dad had been the worst day of his life.

Everyone had known Peter Simmons to be a fun-loving and wonderful man. Thinking Jaris needed a mother, he'd remarried three times, all of the marriages ending in divorce after a couple of years or less.

On Jaris's sixteenth birthday, his dad asked him what he wanted. Jaris had answered he didn't need anything, including a new mother. "You're the only parent I need, Dad."

His dad had given him one of his big bear hugs and had choked back a few "uncommon for him" tears. "Women don't make it with old cops like your dad, son. It's a hard life. Being a cop destroys relationships."

When Jaris had told him that he wanted to be a cop, his dad had asked him to reconsider. Of course, he hadn't. Being a policeman had been in Jaris's very DNA. When he'd graduated from the police academy, his father had smiled with pride.

Losing his sight had been another hard day for Jaris. He couldn't be a cop anymore. Everyone had expected him to go into a deep depression, but he hadn't. He'd found a new life in Destiny. Like his dad, he didn't get bogged down when things turned dark. As his dad had always said, "Never focus on what you can't change, son. Just keep pushing forward. Things will get better."

For the first time in Jaris's life, his dad's words didn't apply.

Things weren't going to get better. While he'd been a cop, Jaris had never dreamed of having a permanent relationship with a woman. Given the track records of the men in his family with women, being single had suited him just fine. But that was before meeting Kaylyn. Now, his entire world was upside down. Trying to remain positive was impossible.

Kaylyn could never be his. She was Chance's. Chance was hers. That was how it was. That was how it should be. Chance was his best friend in the world. He needed to be happy for his friend, and he was, but he was also sad that he would have to love Kaylyn from afar.

I'll always love her.

"Sugar." He swung his legs over the bed, feeling for her lead. Sugar was right there, where he needed her to be. "I need another bottle of wine, and I bet you wouldn't mind having another treat."

He stood and headed into the kitchen, doubting even more wine would help him sleep.

* * * *

Chance sat in Doc's office with Kaylyn, keeping hold of her hand. She was in the wheelchair next to him, and Annie was on the floor on the other side of her.

Jaris had gone over to the sheriff's office to find out what had been discovered about the shooter and the missing dogs. Lyle was taking care of Kaylyn's other dogs up at the Boys Ranch.

Kaylyn squeezed his hand. "I'm so anxious to talk to Doc. What's taking him so long?"

He smiled. "That's the fifth time you've asked that since we got here. Remember, patience is a virtue."

She giggled. "It's been ten minutes. Punctuality is a virtue in my book. I guess I'm anxious about everything, Chance. Our dogs are still missing. I want Doc to get this over with and release me. Then we can join Jaris at the sheriff's office and find out what has been discovered."

Chance doubted she would get a total green light from Doc. She likely needed another day or two before he would release her fully.

The door opened.

"Would either of you like a cup of coffee?" Paris asked.

"Not me, but thanks," he answered. "What about you, honey?

"I'm coffeed out. Paris, how much longer until Doc comes in?" Kaylyn wasn't holding back her frustration. Not surprising, since she and Paris were close friends.

"Dustin is on the phone." Paris was one of the few residents of Destiny who sometimes referred to Doc by his given name. "He'll be in here any minute. Sorry for the delay."

"It's okay." Kaylyn's tone softened. "I'm just worried about my dogs. It's put me on edge."

"Jason will find them. He's got the whole town looking."

"That does make me feel a little better. Thanks. Chance and I are going over to Jason's office. Jaris is already with him."

"Let me see if I can hurry Dustin up." Paris left.

She was a good nurse and a warm person. Even though he was blind, Chance knew that Paris belonged with Doc and Mick. He just wasn't sure what was keeping them from taking the final plunge.

Who am I to talk? Look how long it took me to confess what I felt for Kaylyn.

Kaylyn sighed. "Do you believe there's something troubling, Jaris?"

He didn't want to worry her. "You do have a lot on your mind this morning." The only thing Jaris was focused on was finding that fucking guy who shot Kaylyn, the same thing that was on his mind, too. "What makes you think he might?"

"Nothing I can put my finger on, but he just seemed a little distant to me." She sighed. "Maybe it's just all in my imagination."

He grabbed her hand and squeezed. "You okay?"

"I've never been happier, honey."

He leaned over and kissed her. "I love you."

Last night had been incredible. She'd fallen asleep in his arms, and he'd stayed awake for a little bit longer than she had, enjoying the feel of her body next to his.

He heard the door open again.

"Good morning," Doc said. "How are you feeling today, Kaylyn?"

"I'm fine. I have some questions for you."

"Let me take a look at your leg before we get into those, okay?"

"Fine."

Chance grinned, knowing how impatient she could be.

"Excellent. Looks great. You and Jaris did good taking care of my patient."

"Our pleasure, Doc."

"I've got to sing tonight at the opening ceremony for Dragon Week. Can you give me a release, please?"

"I'd like you to keep completely off your leg for the rest of the day. After that, it's okay to walk and do normal activities, but absolutely no working with dogs."

"What? That's my job, Doc."

"Not for at least a week it isn't."

"That's impossible. I have things I must do. Sammie is about to deliver pups. I have dogs halfway through their training that need to continue. And I still must find my other four dogs."

Chance could hear the anxiety in her tone. "Sweetheart, Lyle is taking care of Annie and the other dogs. Jason hasn't stopped looking for Rex, Blue, King, and Rosie. He won't stop until they are found. There's nothing you need to do but listen to Doc."

"Fine, but I don't have to like what he has to say."

Doc laughed. "No you don't. If any of your dogs jumped on you and opened your wound, we'd be back to square one. About your performance tonight, as long as your band lets you sit onstage, I don't see a problem with it."

"Don't worry about that, Doc," Chance said, putting his arm around Kaylyn. "We'll make sure she follows all your orders."

"Tyrants." Kaylyn laughed. "Fine. What about sex, Doc? How long do I have to wait before I have sex?"

Chance grinned but wanted to know, too. One thing about Kaylyn, she wasn't afraid to speak her mind.

"You're free to have sex but just don't put pressure on your leg."

"That's the best news I've heard all day." Kaylyn's excited tone made him happy.

He could feel his cock begin to stir. "Doc, I'll make sure of that, too."

* * * *

"None of this is adding up." With Sugar at his feet, Jaris sat across from Jason Wolfe in his office. "The fucker shot Kaylyn, Sheriff."

"Yes, he did." Wolfe was a good lawman. He'd found the shooter and had him and his buddies in custody. The bastard, a Dr. Leland Potter from Salt Lake City, was just down the hall in a cell, not thirty feet from where he and Jason were now. "Potter acted shocked during the interrogation, though I'm not buying it. All five of them said they didn't realize they were on private property."

"Bullshit. I know that the Stones have their property clearly posted everywhere."

"There are a lot of roads into their land, Jaris. It's one of the largest ranches in Swanson County. Nicole checked out the cattle guard the doctors claimed to have driven through. The sign was missing."

"Did you check their trucks for the sign?"

"We did. Nothing. Each of them passed the breathalyzer test, too."

"So they want us to believe that five doctors went on a coyote hunting trip together to bond with each other, and just accidently ended up on Stone Ranch, and somehow got lost, and Potter's gun accidently went off, and Kaylyn got shot, and none of them saw her, or us, or our missing dogs? Bullshit. I'm the one who's blind, not those fuckers, right?"

"All good points, Jaris. I don't believe Potter and his buddies were hunting coyote, but I don't have any proof. Being physicians, they have a team of high-paid lawyers who have already contacted me. The slimeballs are already on their way to Destiny to make sure their clients get released ASAP. Even though they were trespassing, I don't have enough to hold Potter's buddies, but I can keep him in the tank until his attorney arrives. After that, I will have to release him, too. All five will have to go to court, but Ethel has set Potter's court date for next week, so he will have to remain in town even if he makes bail. A small consolation, but it's all we have at the moment."

Jaris heard the door open.

"Hey, Kaylyn," the sheriff said. "How are you doing?"

"I'm much better, Jason. Do you know anything about my four dogs?"

The sound of her voice warmed Jaris all over. Listening, Jaris heard the squeak from Kaylyn's wheelchair and the footsteps of Chance with Annie. He'd left them alone again this morning. It was the right thing to do, though it had felt like a punch in the gut.

They belong together, Jaris. Don't fuck things up. You care about both of them.

He took a deep breath, trying to push down his pain.

"Still no sign of them, I'm sorry to say."

"Honey, it's going to be okay." Chance placed Kaylyn's wheelchair between Jaris and the empty chair. Chance took the seat, keeping her between them. "What about the shooter?"

"I was just filling in Jaris about what we know so far. We have the man who shot you in custody. Him and his friends."

The sheriff repeated what he'd already told him about the five doctors.

"My dogs couldn't have just vanished into thin air." Kaylyn's voice trembled slightly with worry and frustration. "None of this makes any sense."

"I agree, and so does Jaris." Sheriff Wolfe had one of the toughest jobs in the entire state, and yet he continued to be there for the citizens of Destiny in every way. "My gut tells me that Lunceford has something to do with this whole thing."

"I know the creep is after Belle, but I don't know why he would want me shot. And what do my dogs have to do with anything?"

"That's what I intend to find out, Kaylyn."

The more time Jaris was around the sheriff the more he liked and respected the man. "Jason, those four dogs have been highly trained. If they weren't dead or injured, they would've returned to the ranch. Someone took them. Chance and I did hear them yelp."

"I remember you saying that." Jason tapped his pencil on the surface of his desk. "I think the key is finding Kaylyn's dogs. Once we do, we might discover some link to the doctors. If those five did take the dogs, they couldn't have stashed them far. We'll find them, Kaylyn. I promise."

"I'd like to interrogate the doctors. Ask Nicole. I was one of the best at getting perps to confess back in Chicago."

"You know what, I think that's a good idea. I've been meaning to deputize you both. Once you take the oath, it'll be official and you can interrogate your ass off, Jaris."

"You're kidding, right?" Chance was clearly as surprised as he was. "Jaris and I are blind. What kind of deputies would we make?"

"It's Dragon Week. There are a ton of outsiders in Destiny for the event. I need you. With or without your eyes, you two are massive and intimidating. Add Sugar and Annie to the mix and nobody is going to mess with you. Plus, both of you see more than most with your other senses."

"Sheriff, are you sure?" Jaris reached in his jacket pocket and touched the handle of his ever-present gun. It had been ages since he fired it.

"More than sure. You'll be given radios. If there's anything you need backup on, Nicole and I will be right there."

"We'll I'm not convinced," Chance said.

"Maybe these will help both of you." The sheriff opened one of his desk drawers. "These are your badges."

Jaris wrapped his fingers around the shield and smiled.

"Seriously, Jason. I'm willing to help you in any way I can, but I can't carry a badge, even a deputy sheriff's badge."

"Really, Chance? You and Jaris saved Kaylyn. You acted quickly and responsibly. You gave us the clues, which resulted in us bringing in Potter and his gang. Sounds like good police work to me. Does it to you?"

"It feels good to have a badge in my hand, Sheriff." Jaris turned to Chance. "Buddy, you are capable of so much. Besides, being deputies will allow us a leg up on keeping Kaylyn safe."

"I hadn't thought of that."

"Chance, I know you and Jaris would make wonderful additions to Destiny's law enforcement team." Kaylyn's voice was full of pride and admiration.

Jaris imagined she was looking at Chance and smiling. When he felt her grab his hand, warmth spread through him.

Keep your head. She belongs with Chance, not you.

"If Kaylyn and Jaris both think we can do the job, who am I to stand in the way?" Chance laughed. "When do we start?"

"Right away. Raise your right hands, gentlemen, and repeat after me."

Taking the oath of office, Jaris's life had come full circle. He was going to be a cop again. That miracle should've been enough to satisfy him, but it wasn't. He inhaled Kaylyn's scent and knew nothing would be enough for him ever again. Didn't matter. Even if he didn't get his heart's desire, she and Chance would be happy together. That had to suffice.

Chapter Seven

In the wheelchair next to Chance, Kaylyn stared through the one-way glass into the interrogation room. The man sitting in the metal chair at the table seemed cocky. He had a receding hairline. He looked to be in his midforties. Slim stature. Dark eyes.

This is my shooter.

She trembled, wondering if he was somehow connected to Lunceford. Maybe Potter's and his friends' stories were true. Maybe everything that happened had been just an accident of poor timing and judgment.

That didn't explain Rex, Blue, King, and Rosie still being missing. Where were they? So many questions and not enough answers.

Chance touched her cheek. "You doing okay?"

"Yes, but I'm ready to hear what this guy has to say." She sighed, closing her eyes. Answers. That's what she needed and fast.

"Me, too."

Doc had told her she couldn't work with dogs for a week. Even if the four were found today, she wouldn't be able to help Jaris and Chance with their final training. "I'm going to have to call the new owners and tell them we don't have their dogs ready."

"Sweetheart, don't lose faith. We'll figure it all out together. If they have to wait a few days longer, that's not a big deal."

"But if we don't find the dogs, they'll have to wait at least three months for us to get four more dogs up to par."

"We'll find them. You'll see. Jaris will find out the truth. Maybe even today. I have all the confidence in him in the world."

"I do too, Chance."

The sheriff marched into the interrogation room with Jaris, who had Sugar by his side.

Dr. Potter sat up straight, staring at the black German shepherd with wide eyes. "Why is this dog here?"

"Relax, Doctor," the sheriff said. "My associate is blind. This is his service dog. You have nothing to fear."

Kaylyn knew better. If Potter made any threatening move toward Jaris, Sugar would rip the guy apart.

Jaris reached out with a trembling hand, acting as if he was completely helpless, which she definitely knew he wasn't. "Where's my chair, Sheriff?"

Jason took Jaris's wrist and moved his hand to the back of the chair. "Here it is, Deputy."

"Deputy?" Potter looked back and forth from the sheriff to Jaris. "What kind of crazy town is this?"

"It's my town, Doctor. This is Deputy Simmons."

Jaris smiled, taking a seat directly across from the man. "I can understand why you think it's strange. Destiny isn't like anywhere else in the world. The citizens here take chances on people like me. Stay a little while and this place will grow on you. It has on me."

She smiled, liking how Jaris described her hometown. It was unique and special, just like him.

"It would be easier to like if I weren't in jail, Deputy."

"I agree. Once we get to the bottom of this, perhaps you won't have to stay in here any longer." Jaris's demeanor was warm and charming. It was clear he was trying to break the ice with Potter, to get on the man's good side. Very impressive. Though she'd worked with him training dogs for some time now, she'd never seen this part of him before. He must've been quite the detective prior to losing his sight. "Before we get started, would you like something to drink?"

Potter smiled broadly. "I sure would. I'm trying to keep my weight down. Do you have Diet Coke, Sheriff?"

Jason nodded, stood, and left the room.

"What's your background, Deputy? Your boss asked me and my friends a bunch of questions. That cute deputy did, too. What was her name?"

Nicole.

"Doesn't matter, Dr. Potter." Jaris smiled, patting Sugar on the head. "I just have a few things to ask you. That's all."

"Like what?"

"I hear you came to Colorado to hunt. Could you tell me about that?"

Potter went into great detail about how he and his friends had come up with the trip. They'd learned that you didn't have to have a license to hunt coyotes in the state. They'd bagged three.

The sheriff returned with a Diet Coke and placed it in front of their prisoner.

"Thank you." Potter popped the top and took a drink.

Jaris continued questioning the guy, clearly probing for cracks in his story.

"Jaris is doing a great job." Chance placed his arm around her shoulder. "I bet the guy is sweating bullets by now."

She stared directly at the man. "Not yet. Potter doesn't seem rattled one bit. Everything he's saying sounds reasonable to me. Maybe this is just an unfortunate turn of circumstances and has nothing to do with Kip Lunceford."

"Doctor, when your gun misfired, what did you hear?"

"I don't know what you're getting at, Deputy."

"You were out in nature. There are plenty of noises. What did you hear?"

"Birds, mostly."

"Anything else?"

"A waterfall. We parked both our trucks near it."

"Where were your friends when your gun went off."

"By the trucks."

"And you?"

Potter shrugged. "A little bit away from them. I'm not sure how far."

"Five feet? Ten? Thirty? Approximately how far?"

"A hundred yards, maybe. Like I said, I'm not sure."

"Did you hear anything else?"

"No." Potter leaned back in his chair, going on and on about how much he enjoyed hunting.

"What kind of medicine do you practice in Salt Lake?" Jaris's question seemed to stump the man, as his eyes narrowed.

In an even tone, Potter answered, "I'm just a regular doctor, Deputy."

"We sure need more of those. What about your four friends? Do they specialize in anything?"

"Go, Jaris," Chance whispered, even though he couldn't be heard in the other room. "You're onto something."

She agreed. Potter's face was tight. What was the man hiding?

Potter shook his head. "You'll need to ask them, Deputy. We don't share patients."

Suddenly, Jaris switched gears, asking all sorts of unrelated questions. Was Potter married? Kids? How long had he practiced in Utah? Had he practiced anywhere else?

Potter's answers were short and to the point. It was clear that the man was clamming up. Jaris was getting to him.

"What medical school did you go to, Doctor?"

Potter frowned and turned to the sheriff. "I've answered all your questions and still you keep grilling me. I feel awful that someone got shot because of my gun misfiring, but I'm not a criminal. I've answered all the questions I'm going to answer until my attorney arrives. That's within my rights, isn't it?"

"Relax, Doctor." The sheriff stood. "We're only trying to make sure we report everything accurately."

"Just doing our jobs." Jaris also stood. "You've been most helpful, Dr. Potter. Thank you for your cooperation on this."

Potter smiled, the lines in his face softening. "You're very welcome, Deputy. Tell me, how is the woman doing? She's okay, isn't she?"

Jaris's eyes narrowed slightly for a brief second. "She's in good hands."

* * * *

Sitting in her wheelchair, Kaylyn waited in the band's trailer for the show to start. She took a sip of water and blew out a deep breath.

"You don't have to go on tonight, Kaylyn." Mitchell was the leader of Wolfe Mayhem. He was also a good friend. Mitchell was Jason and Lucas's brother. The three Wolfe brothers were happily engaged to Phoebe.

"I told you. Doc gave his blessing. I just have to stay seated. I'll wheel myself out in this chair."

"You won't be wheeling yourself out." Chance stroked her hair. "I will."

"And Chance and I will be next to the stage, ready for anything." Jaris, like Chance, had become even more protective of her ever since the interrogation of Potter. Still, his demeanor had seemed off somehow since last night. "The first sign of trouble and you're coming off the stage."

She shook her head. "Nothing is going to go wrong." But something was definitely wrong with Jaris.

"We have everything under control." Chance placed his hand on her shoulder. "Jaris and I will do whatever we have to do to keep you safe from Potter and his buddies."

"All those guys made bail," Mitchell said. "Any word from Jena and her guys about what they've found on the information highway about them?"

"So far, everything lines up with what they've said." Jaris leaned down and rubbed Sugar's back. "But I know Potter is hiding something. The way his voice stiffened when I asked him about his practice tells me he's lying. If anyone can get to the truth, it's Jena."

Kaylyn looked at Mitchell. "Seriously, I'm fine. I want to sing. Jason is keeping a detail near Potter and his friend during the whole evening."

"I heard. Nicole is leading some of the team and Dylan the others." Mitchell smiled. "Add to them Chance, Annie, Jaris, and Sugar on the job, any of those five doctors make a wrong move and they'll be sorry they did."

Hank, the band's lead guitarist, came into the trailer. "We're on in five, you two."

"We're ready." She turned to Chance. "You really want to wheel me out?"

"I do." He grabbed the handles of her chair.

Hank held the door open.

"Hold on," Jaris said firmly.

"Don't try to talk me out of this." *What is up with him?* "Everything is going to be okay. I promise."

He bent down and touched her on the shoulder. "Keep your eyes on the crowd. You see anything that doesn't seem right, just say 'I see a cowboy out there.' That will tip me and Chance to get you off the stage."

"That's a great idea, Jaris," Mitchell said. "I'll keep my eyes peeled, too. If need be, I'll pull the plug and help you get Kaylyn back to the trailer."

She reached up and touched Jaris on the cheek. His stubble tickled her fingertips. "I promise. Now, can Chance take me to the stage?"

Jaris stepped back and his bearing turned dark and withdrawn again. "Yes. Let's get her out there."

She didn't have time to ask him about it now, but she was determined to ask him at home tonight. Chance pulled her into his big arms and carried her down the three short steps. Mitchell lugged the wheelchair through the door and Chance settled her back down. He pushed her toward the stage.

Like everyone in Destiny, Kaylyn loved Dragon Week. It was one of her favorite events of the year.

She glanced over at the O'Leary family, the founders of Dragon Week and the town's most loved trio. All three were in their eighties, but their advanced age didn't slow them down one bit. They were vibrant, charming, and full of life. Though they were the richest family in Destiny, with an extreme wealth into the billions, they were the most generous and down-to-earth people she'd ever known. Patrick O'Leary, the Master of Ceremony and dragon expert, sat next to his wife. Ethel, who still was the county's judge, looked gorgeous with her silver hair neat as always. Ethel's other husband, Sam O'Leary, stood behind them, holding a walkie-talkie in his hand. Even at his age, Sam, like many of the locals, had volunteered for the event's security team, which was double from last year. Had to be, since Lunceford was still on the loose.

Thinking about Destiny's most evil enemy, Kaylyn trembled. Were Jaris and Chance right about her shooter? Did Potter have some connection to Lunceford? If so, did the bastard have her four precious dogs?

The stage was dimly lit but would be washed in light once Patrick introduced the band.

"How are you doing?" Big Jim, who played rhythm guitar for Wolfe Mayhem, looked at her with concern all over his face.

Godric, their British bass player, stood next to Big Jim with the same look.

"I'm doing much better. It's only a flesh wound. That's not going to keep me down." She turned her head to Chance. "A little to the left and you'll have me right at my microphone. That's perfect. Thank you."

He locked the brakes of the wheelchair and came to the side of her. "Sweetheart, I love you."

Utter joy filled her entire being. How long had she wanted to hear him say those three precious words to her? Since last night he'd said them many times. "I love you, too."

He pressed his lips to hers, causing butterflies to take flight inside her. "Jaris and I will be only steps away. Use your eyes. Say those words."

She grinned, loving how protective he and Jaris were being with her. They made her feel so safe. "I remember. I'm to say 'I see a cowboy out there.'"

"That's my girl."

She reached down and patted Annie. "Unless you and your master want to be part of the show, girl, you better lead him off the stage."

Another kiss, and then Chance moved away.

Her eyes wandered over the crowd, which was clearly bigger than last year. Dragon Week continued to grow and grow. There were people here from around the country and the world. There were attendees from as far away as China, Nepal, Australia, South Africa, and more.

She spotted familiar faces. Nicole and her two husbands, Sawyer and Reed. The three were obviously keeping watch for any sign of trouble. On the front row was one of Kaylyn's dearest friends, Paris. Paris sat with some other locals, but there was no sign of Doc or Mick Ryder. Kaylyn wanted her friend to find love, like she had just yesterday.

A spotlight came on, illuminating the O'Learys. The crowd went nuts, coming to their feet and cheering. The energy was incredible.

Patrick held a microphone. "Welcome, believers."

More applause.

Godric stepped next to her, and in his typical British accent said, "This is quite the party, isn't it, Kaylyn?"

"Yes, it is." Like her, he was new to the band. Unlike her, this was his first time at Dragon Week.

Patrick continued with the introductions, explaining some of the things that would be happening over the week.

She closed her eyes, getting her mind settled on the set they'd picked out for tonight's performance. She loved singing almost as much as she loved training her dogs.

When she opened her eyes, her heart nearly stopped when she spotted her shooter sitting five rows back in the audience. She was about to say the words that would bring Chance and Jason running, when she saw who was right behind Potter. Jason and Dylan.

She took a deep, calming breath.

Patrick continued, "Please put your hands together and welcome, Wolfe Mayhem."

Mitchell hit the snare three times, setting the beat.

She began singing their opening number.

Chapter Eight

Kaylyn stared at Jaris standing by her front door with Sugar. "I've already talked to Belle. You don't have to go check on the boys."

Chance sat next to her with Annie at their feet. "Buddy, you should listen to her. You know how she likes to get her way."

Jaris laughed halfheartedly. "I'm leaving her in good hands. She'll be fine."

Kaylyn wasn't ready to give up the fight. "Belle, Corey, and Shane have been taking over yours and Chance's duties since my accident. The boys are fine, Jaris. I'd like you to stay here."

"I appreciate the Stone's help, but it's my job, not theirs."

"Hey, buddy. It's both our jobs."

Jaris shook his head, a sign that he hadn't been born blind. "I know, but one of us has to stay here to protect her. Jason has assigned several deputies to keep tabs on things around her house, but we both know that someone has to be inside with her. Remember, she can't put any pressure on her leg until tomorrow. So, that job falls to you."

"A job I'll gladly take."

Jaris smiled. "I'll spend the night at the ranch and take care of the boys. I'll see you at the next Dragon Week event tomorrow. Emmett will be here in just a second. I need to get going."

Something about the way he'd been acting the last twenty-four hours, including now, didn't sit well with her. "What's really the matter, Jaris? You don't seem like yourself."

He sighed but didn't say anything for a moment.

"Please. Talk to me." She heard a honk.

"That's Emmett. We can talk tomorrow, Kaylyn. You and Chance have a nice evening."

Jaris walked out with Sugar, shutting the door behind him.

She closed her eyes tight, hurting deep inside. "Chance, he's holding back something. I can tell he's struggling."

"I believe you might be right, but what is he struggling with?"

She grabbed Chance's hand. "I was hoping you could shed some light on it. You're his friend. Do you have any idea what it might be?"

"Not really, but don't worry, sweetheart. We'll talk to him about it tomorrow." Chance leaned over and pressed his lips to hers, sending a wonderful shiver up and down her spine.

Without warning, Chance stood and lifted her out of the wheelchair. "I thought you might be ready to get out of your chariot."

She looked into his chocolate eyes. "Past ready."

"Would you like to go to the bedroom or just sit on the sofa for a little while? And I do mean for a *little while*. I've already determined our final destination for tonight, sweetheart."

She grinned. "Why, Mr. Reynolds, aren't you being forward?"

He kissed her again, making her dizzy with want. He traced her lips with his tongue. "It's just the beginning, baby. I've waited a long time to hold you in my arms. There's much more to come."

"I would like to experience whatever you have in mind. I'm sure it will be wonderful." Her body was warm. She wanted him from the top of her head to the tip of her toes—and everywhere in between. She'd dreamed about being with him since their kiss under the mistletoe. "Let's continue this in the bedroom."

"You've got a deal, baby."

Gazing at his handsome face, she wrapped her arms around his neck. "You're quite the kisser, Mr. Reynolds."

"And so are you, Miss Anderson." He brought his mouth to hers once again, claiming her with his lips.

When he ended the kiss, she found it hard to catch her breath as he carried her to the bedroom. He lowered her gently down onto the bed and began unbuttoning her shirt.

"I've waited so long to feel your body, Kaylyn." Chance's words sounded deep and so very intense, making her tingle.

"I want you to see all of me with your touch, honey."

With her shirt agape, he stretched out beside her on the bed. He didn't bring his hands to her breasts at first, but touched her face instead, tracing every line, seeing her in his way.

"You're so beautiful, Kaylyn. The most beautiful woman in the world."

She smiled, looking at his ebony skin. "My face hasn't changed much since you last touched it."

"Still beautiful, but I'm touching you with my heart completely open now, baby. It's different. Wonderful. Overwhelming. I love you, Kaylyn."

"I love you." She closed her eyes, as he caressed her body.

He ran his fingers down her neck slowly. Tingles spread through her body and she felt her heart begin to speed up in her chest.

He brought his lips to where his hands had just visited, tasting the skin on her neck. "I need to see every inch of your body, sweetheart."

He removed her shirt and kissed her shoulders.

"I love the way you *look* at me, Chance."

His fingers continued down her body with his lips falling close behind. As his hands traced her arms, warmth washed over her.

In a flash, he had her out of her bra, leaving her breasts completely exposed.

He touched them tenderly. "They're beautiful, like I knew they would be."

When he bent down and kissed her nipples, she felt electricity shoot from where his lips connected to her skin all the way down to her pussy, which began to ache.

With his tongue, he circled her tiny buds, which were tightening. Mad with want, she shivered as he moved his hands down her stomach, stopping just short of where she needed his touch the most.

Liquid began seeping out of her pussy and her clit began to throb.

Chance kissed his way down her stomach.

"Feels so good. So good." She fisted the sheet as he continued exploring her body.

He removed the rest of her clothes, tossing them to the floor.

"My God, you're incredible." He kissed her thighs, placing his hands under her, massaging her ass.

She couldn't contain herself and began to moan.

Her desire for him to ease the expanding pressure inside her was maddening as he slowly caressed most of her body but never grazed her most intimate spot. "Please, Chance. Touch my pussy. Please. I beg you."

"I will, sweetheart. Be patient. It will make your pleasure all the more satisfying for you." He ran his hands down her leg, being careful of her injury. "Your body is so perfect, sweetheart." He ripped off his shirt, revealing his chocolate, muscled chest.

She let her gaze wander over him, taking in his ultimate abs. "Yours is too, honey. I've never seen anyone so ripped before."

He grinned. "You're about to see more of me."

He took off the rest of his clothes, and what she saw nearly took her breath away. His cock was quite thick and so very long.

"Chance, I have some protection in my dresser drawer."

"You do?"

She brought her hands up to his chest. "It's always been for you."

He smiled. "We don't need it quite yet." He crawled up between her legs. "I've got something else in mind."

When his fingers threaded through her wet folds, she gasped. The pressure continued to build and build. She'd desired him for so long, it was going to be impossible to go slow.

He ran his hands over her pussy, taking in every inch with tender touches.

When he applied just the right pressure on her swollen folds, she felt her whole body shake and she pounded her fists on the mattress. She was practically melting. "Oh God. Yes. More. Oh. Faster. Please."

"No, baby. I want this nice and slow." He pressed his lips to her pussy. "You know what they say about the blind's senses. I've touched you. Now, I want to taste you." With his tongue he began licking her into a complete state of frenzy. She draped her legs over his shoulders.

He laved her pussy, and the pressure became almost unbearable. The more he drank from her body the wetter she became.

"You taste so sweet, Kaylyn. I love every drop." He fingered her anus while lapping up her juices.

Writhing like crazy, she clutched the back of his head, pushing him deeper into her pussy.

When he applied pressure to her clit with his lips, she couldn't contain herself any longer.

Her body erupted as the massive pressure inside her released into a sea of sensations, hot and electric. Her skin burned and her body vibrated. Her pussy began to spasm, clenching and unclenching, again and again. Over and over.

Every wave that crashed inside her made her scream his name. "Chance. Oh God. Chance."

"Yes, baby. I'm here." He moved up her body and held her tenderly. "I'll always be here with you."

She could feel his erection pressing against her, causing the pressure to return. "I need you inside me, Chance." She ran her hands over his chest and abs. "I desperately need to feel you."

"I want that, too, sweetheart. I want you so very much. I've wanted you for a very long time."

"We both have." She reached for the box of condoms in her nightstand, and saw the sprig of mistletoe she'd saved from long ago.

The miracle had finally happened. Chance loved her. She pulled out one foil package and checked the expiration date. Thankfully, it was still good.

She tore the package open and placed the rubber on him. It was a snug fit given the massiveness of his cock. Still she was able to roll it down his shaft.

"That feels so good, baby." His tone deepened, vibrating along her skin.

She fisted him, but was unable to bring her fingers together around his cock. She trembled at the idea of such a large dick penetrating her pussy.

Chance rolled onto his back, keeping his hands on her body, placing her on top of him. "Let's start this way."

Wanting to pleasure him, she grabbed hold of his cock. She shifted her body until her pussy was rubbing against the tip of his dick. She closed her eyes, dropping down on his cock an inch at a time.

She'd never been stretched so much in all her life. "I want every last inch of you in my body."

His breathing was labored. "I want that, too."

She could tell he was on edge, ready to unleash his beast, his lust, his dominance. His willpower amazed her. But she was out of control and wanted him to be, too. She needed him to take her, to ravish her, to claim her for all time.

She slammed her body all the way down his shaft and screamed, as his cock rubbed against her G-spot.

Chance grabbed her by the waist and began thrusting his cock in and out of her pussy. She clawed at his chest, riding every plunge, enjoying the feel of him inside her body. In and out.

"Oh God, Chance. Yes. Yes. Yes." Another orgasm consumed her, sending her into a state of bliss and oblivion.

He sent his dick deep into her pussy and she felt his entire body stiffen. He groaned loudly, and she felt his cock pulsing inside her body. Her pussy tightened around his shaft again and again.

She fell down on top of him and he wrapped his arms around her. Their breaths seemed to synchronize as they remained in that position for a few moments.

"Chance, that was so incredible. Why did we wait so long to be honest with one another?"

"Because I was a fool. But no more. We have years of catching up to do, sweetheart." He kissed her hair. "And I plan on making all of them up to you."

She wanted to pleasure him with her mouth as he'd done her.

Rolling off of him, she reached down and removed the condom. He was semihard. She wrapped her hand around his shaft.

Chance laughed lustily. "I like where this is going, baby, but be careful of your leg, okay?"

She kissed him. "I will."

"Good. Now, show me what your pretty mouth can do."

She wrapped her fingers around his cock, licking its head. He began to get hard. His dick grew in her hands to its full length again.

Cupping his heavy balls, she traced up and down his shaft with her tongue. His groans told her he was enjoying her oral treatment.

"Swallow me, sweetheart." Chance sounded so forceful and dominant. Though she knew he'd never been to Phase Four, the local BDSM club, she could imagine he would fit in quite nicely. "Let me feel your throat tightening around my cock."

"Yes, Sir." The response seemed so natural and appropriate to her. She loved him and respected him. He deserved everything she could give him.

She circled the head of his cock one more time before taking it into her mouth. Relaxing the back of her throat, she took as much of him as she could.

"Yes, sweetheart. That's it. Perfect."

She bobbed up and down his dick, hollowing out her cheeks as she sucked hard on him. Her blonde hair hung down her face, hitting his chocolate skin. She felt his hands on the sides of her face. He was *watching* her.

Up and down, she sucked on him, feeling his pulse from his dick to her lips.

"I'm close, baby. So close."

That spurred her on more and she increased her tempo.

"Yes. God. Oh. Fuck." He thrust his cock deeper down her throat and she breathed through her nose, not wanting to waste a single drop of his manly liquid.

He shot his warm load and she drank all of it.

She collapsed beside him as they both tried to catch their breaths. She couldn't stop touching his muscled frame, so she ran her fingers up and down his body again and again.

"How's your leg, sweetheart?"

"It's fine. Why do you ask?"

"I just need a second before we go again."

"What? You've already come twice."

He kissed her. "Like I said before, we have a lot of catching up to do. I want to make love to you all night. You do have more condoms, don't you?"

"I do. I saved them for you."

"I don't understand."

"I bought that box about a week before the Christmas party where we kissed."

"Under the mistletoe?"

"Yes. I had hoped things would go another way than they did."

He sighed. "Baby, that's all my fault."

"No." She ran her finger down his strong jawline. "We both misread each other. We both made mistakes."

"But that's behind us now." He kissed her tenderly. "Wait until next Christmas. I'm putting up mistletoe everywhere. Your lips won't be safe from me ever again. Hell, your body won't be safe. Hold on. How old are those condoms?"

"Don't worry. I checked the expiration date. They're still good."

"Even if they weren't, it's too late to worry about it now." Another kiss from him sent her to the moon. "I'm going to buy a new box tomorrow. Hand me another package, please."

"We're going again so soon?"

"Yes, we're going again right now. You do things to me I've never experienced before."

She felt warm all over. "And you do the same to me, Chance. Is it because we're in love?"

"Yes, baby. I love you so much."

* * * *

Chance stroked Kaylyn's locks, which felt like silk. "I can't get enough of you, sweetheart."

"Same here, honey." She handed him another condom. "Can you be on top this time?"

"I'm not so sure about that." He was worried about injuring her leg in that position.

"Why not?"

"Baby, Doc said you could have sex but he also said to be careful." He inhaled deeply, filling his nostrils with her scent, which reminded him of orange blossoms in the spring. Her aroma drove him mad with desire, and he felt his cock begin to harden again.

"I love how you take care of me, Chance. But it will be okay."

He smiled, donning the condom. "With you under me I could become a wild man."

"My wound is on the outside of my leg. So, I'll wrap my legs around you, and that way they won't touch anything. Besides, I wouldn't mind experiencing your wild side, Mr. Reynolds."

God, he loved how fiery she was being. Her flame was causing his pulse to burn through every vein. "Is that right, Miss Anderson?"

"Absolutely."

He gave her a deep lingering kiss, enjoying the taste of her lips. Like honey. Sweet and delicious. Gently, he lifted her legs over his shoulders. She bent her knees down his back.

He ran his hands up and down her soft skin, finally resting his hands on her full mounds. She was beautiful. He licked her neck, inhaling more of her intoxicating fragrance. Hearing her little moans of delight was like heaven.

"Your leg okay, baby?"

"I'm doing great, Chance. Please. Make love to me again. I beg you."

Her pleas drove him insane with lust. He carefully moved until his cock was pressing on her tight little pussy.

He thrust into her body, enjoying the feel of her tightening around his cock with her wet depths. "Oh God, Kaylyn. You feel so good."

"So do you, honey. So do you."

He felt her place her delicate fingers on the side of his face, which spurred him on.

With each thrust of his cock into her body, he claimed her as his own. In and out.

Another thrust. "You." And another. "Are." And one more. "Mine."

"Yes. I'm yours. All yours, my love."

He could feel her trembles against his skin. Increasing his tempo, he sent his dick again and again into her body, stretching her pussy.

Hearing her pants and moans, Chance knew he was satisfying her needs, which sparked even more hunger inside him. He plunged deeper and harder into her.

Over and over. Again and again. Harder and faster.

Time had no meaning to him, as their lovemaking transported him to a state of utter abandon.

She's mine.

"Oh God, Chance. Yes. Yes. Yes."

"Come for me, baby. That's it." He felt her pussy tighten hard around his dick, and he thrust one last time into her body. Releasing into Kaylyn again, he realized the woman of his dreams had been right in front of him all along. Now, at long last, his future with her was beginning.

Chapter Nine

Kaylyn gazed at Chance, who was still naked next to her, leaning on his elbow and touching her face with his other hand. "Are you hungry?"

"I am and I bet you are, too." He sat up. "What would you like me to get you?"

"Wait. What time is it?" She grinned, because she already knew.

He retrieved his watch and punched the button.

The digital voice announced, "The time is 2:11 a.m."

"So, as of now, it's tomorrow." She giggled. "Doc said I can walk, so I'm going to make something for us."

"Not so fast, sweetheart. I'm sure he meant in the morning."

"It is morning. Your watch just said so."

"You and I both know what Doc meant. Now, tell me what you want to eat, and I will get it."

"But you're not the cook. Jaris is."

"Apparently you've never had one of my world-renowned peanut butter sandwiches."

"Okay, Mr. Reynolds. You win now, but tomorrow, I am going to walk."

"That's something I love about you, baby. Your fire and will."

She smiled. "I'd love one of your world-renowned peanut butter sandwiches with a tall glass of milk."

"Coming right up." He stood, leaving the mattress.

She drank in his naked body, which was the most beautiful thing she'd ever seen in her life. "Don't forget about Annie, Chance. She might want a treat."

"I bet she does. She also likes peanut butter." He patted his leg and Annie came running. "We'll be right back, sweetheart."

They left her alone and she pulled the covers up to her chin. She was completely spent and relished every bit of it. Chance had made love to her in ways she'd never dreamed possible. She was pretty sure he would be open to the BDSM lifestyle she craved.

She loved him so much, but something still seemed to be missing. *Not something. Someone. Jaris. Why did he leave so suddenly?*

She sat up in the bed. Jaris had captured her heart shortly after coming to work with her. He was kind and genuine. Heroic in every way. He was good to the orphan boys and had a kind spirit. He was also tough and dependable. He made her laugh.

I love Jaris, too. That was the truth. Her truth.

Can Chance accept that? She wasn't sure.

I love them both.

But Chance wasn't from Destiny. Neither was Jaris. *I don't know if Jaris feels the same way about me.* What if being honest ruined what she had with Chance? What if Jaris didn't feel the same way about her? Questions swirled in her head like angry bees, each with a painful sting ready.

"But I can't hold back these feelings," she whispered aloud. How long had she buried her feelings for Chance? Years. She wasn't willing to go through that again. *Whatever happens, I have to tell Chance everything, and later Jaris.*

Part of her wanted to put it off and wait for another time, but she knew what a slippery slope that could be. Days would turn to months and then years, and the truth would remain buried under mounds of doubt and fear.

She closed her eyes, determined to put all her cards on the table when Chance returned with her sandwich. *Tonight, not a minute longer.*

* * * *

It had been a long day. The boys were all in bed, and Jaris quietly shut the door to the dorm room.

Working at the Boys Ranch meant the world to him. He'd never dreamed of having children of his own, but he felt strongly for these boys. Most had been through hell, being moved from one foster family to another. Because of the Stones, they now had a real home.

He wasn't quite ready to call it a night and was pretty sure sleep wouldn't come easy. He had a ton on his mind. He bent down and patted Sugar on the head. She was waiting for him to let her know which direction he wanted to go.

The new building had been designed and built by local architect, Lucas Wolfe, the sheriff's brother. The hallway Jaris was standing in split the place in two sections. On this side were the two giant rooms where the boys slept, one for the older kids and the other for the younger ones. Across the hall was his room, Chance's room, the kitchen and bathrooms. To the right, the hallway led to the front door. To the left, it led to a large rec room, which had sofas, a pool table, and a flat-screen television. Almost every night after getting the boys settled, he and Chance would grab a beer from the fridge and head to the rec room to discuss the day's events.

But Chance isn't here. He is with Kaylyn.

With Sugar, he walked to the kitchen and grabbed a beer. "How about we stretch our legs, girl?"

Sugar led him down the hallway to the front door.

The air outside was crisp. Though he couldn't see the sky, he bet there wasn't a cloud in it.

The dormitory had a wraparound porch with lots of places to sit. He found his favorite chair and sat down. Before he popped the top, he heard footsteps. *Emmett's footsteps.*

"Mind if I join you, Jaris?"

"Actually, I'd like some company. Wanna beer?"

"Yeah."

"They're in the fridge. Help yourself."

"Don't mind if I do." Emmett headed in to retrieve his beer.

The man was as solid as they came. A good friend. Always willing to help and lend an ear.

Jaris popped the top of his beer and took his first sip of the cool liquid. *I could use his advice right now.*

Emmett returned and sat down next to him. "Buddy, what's going on with you?"

Jaris knew the cowboy had good instincts about people but never imagined Emmett could read him so easily. "Is it that obvious?"

"It sure is. You haven't been yourself since Kaylyn was shot. Are you worried about her?"

"Of course I'm worried, Emmett. The creep who shot her is still in town, and until we know for sure that he and his friends aren't connected to Lunceford, I'll remain on guard."

"We're all going to be quite concerned until fucking Lunceford is put away for good." Emmett's sister-in-law's safety was on all their minds. "I know in my gut those so-called hunters are involved. We've got the best sheriff in the state on the job. And don't forget Shannon's Elite is working day and night to capture the bastard, too."

Shannon's Elite was a group of highly trained operatives working for the CIA under the supervision of Easton Black. They were incredibly capable.

Jaris respected the entire team. "But there's more to it than just that." He took another swig of his beer. "I have a lot on my mind."

"Don't forget, buddy. I'm here for you." Emmett was a straight shooter and always meant what he said. Having him in his corner was a very good thing. "I don't want to pry, but I'm ready to listen if you're ready to talk."

"You know how Chance feels about Kaylyn?"

Emmett chuckled. "Everyone in town knows that."

He downed the rest of his beer. "Well, I want to be honest with you. I feel the same way about Kaylyn."

"Oh my God." Emmett slapped him on the back.

"So you see my dilemma. I think I need to leave town."

"What the hell do you mean by that, Jaris? You love her. Chance loves her. What's the damn problem?"

"How can I tell her how I feel when I know she and Chance love each other? They've known each other for ages. I've only known her for less than a year. I can't come between them."

"There's no coming between anybody, Jaris. This is Destiny, not Chicago. We don't put any stops on the people we love. Look at me. My brothers and I love Amber. She's the woman of our dreams and we have the best life imaginable. I love my brothers, and we always wanted to have a family together, just like our parents."

"But Chance and I aren't brothers."

"Oh for God's sakes, Jaris. Everybody knows you are just like brothers. Being brothers is not just from blood. It's what you mean to one another. And there's no doubt in my mind Chance couldn't be more of a brother to you if you had the same parents."

"That's true."

"And you? Willing to leave town just to let him have a chance at a life with Kaylyn. Screwy logic, but I know it comes from your heart. You love him. He *is* your brother."

"Yes, he is." *Is Emmett right? Is it possible that Chance and I could figure a way through this? Can we really share Kaylyn?*

"You're being very selfish, buddy. That's a fact. Have you even thought about asking Kaylyn how she feels? You're one of the best men I have ever met. Hell, you're a goddamn hero. You took a bullet for Nicole. Stop being such a chickenshit. It's time to man up and go talk to her. And you and Chance need to talk. Nothing is ever solved by running away. You just take it with you."

He leaned back in his chair, thinking about all Emmett had said. Chance was his brother. The man had helped him learn to *see* with his other senses. He'd never been as close to another person in his life other than his dad. And what about Kaylyn? She was from Destiny. She'd grown up with two dads.

"I hadn't even considered the possibility that I could share her with Chance, Emmett."

"Not surprising, since you're not from here."

"Actually, I never considered having a family of my own before. The Simmons men have a long history of bad luck when it comes to women. I always thought I'd be a bachelor my whole life."

"Pardon the expression, Jaris. Open your eyes. Happiness might be right in front of you."

"How do you think Chance will feel? He's not from Destiny either."

Emmett stood. "There's only one way to find out."

"You're right. I will talk to both of them tomorrow." Jaris smiled. "Thank you, Emmett. You're a good friend."

"Thanks for the beer."

"Thanks for the advice."

"That's what friends are for, Jaris. Good night."

"Night."

As Emmett walked to the big house, Jaris was starting to believe there might be a happy ending for him in all this after all.

* * * *

Chance felt like he could conquer the world. He'd made love to the woman of his dreams, his best friend in the world. Kaylyn was his. He'd never been happier.

After finishing making the peanut butter sandwiches, he gave Annie a treat. "Good girl." They walked back into Kaylyn's bedroom with their meal. "Dinner is served, my lady."

"Looks delicious. Thank you." Kaylyn's tone was a little muted from when he left her, which surprised him.

They ate their sandwiches quietly. He'd been famished, so he was glad to have some food.

He listened to Kaylyn's breathing, which seemed a little shallow to him, sometimes a sign that something was on her mind. "Sweetheart, would you like to talk?"

She sighed. "We really need to."

He didn't like the sound of worry in her voice. He took her hand. "Whatever it is, I'm here for you. No more secrets between us. Okay?"

"I agree. You know I've been worried about Jaris."

"Me, too. Something is off with him for sure."

"It might be about me."

"Maybe. You were shot. Dealing with that has been all that either he or I have thought about ever since. We want to keep you safe."

"You both have been amazing, but I'm not sure that's all it is. I'm afraid he might've picked up on how I feel about him. That might've put him in an awkward position."

Chance still wasn't sure what Jaris's change of mood was about, but he was beginning to realize what was troubling Kaylyn. "You have feelings for him?"

"Yes," she said softly. "I feel for him like I feel for you."

His gut tightened. "You mean you love him?"

He heard her take a deep breath. "Yes, Chance. I do. I have for some time. You do understand that it doesn't take away my feelings for you?"

"I'm not sure what I understand right now, Kaylyn." He leaned back against the headboard. "I know you're from Destiny and I know what kind of families live here. I just never imagined that was the kind of life you wanted. Now that we're finally together, I was hoping I would be enough."

"Are you angry with me?"

"Of course not, baby. I'm just confused. I didn't grow up here. For me it's always been one man and one woman. Two people building a life together, clinging to each other." He touched her face and felt a tear, which broke his heart. "I love you, Kaylyn, but I don't know if I could share you with anyone."

"It's not that you're not enough, Chance. My heart is big enough for both of you. I've actually dreamed of the three of us together and how wonderful it would be."

"Kaylyn, this is something I have to think about. I need some time."

"I understand."

"Have you told Jaris how you feel about him?"

"No, but I must. I kept my feelings for you secret for so long and it nearly killed me. I won't go through that again. It isn't fair to me or to Jaris, even if he doesn't feel the same way about me."

Chance thought about the possibility of Jaris rejecting Kaylyn, but he knew better. Thinking back about his talks with his best friend, it was clear that Jaris had feelings for Kaylyn, too. He'd never given much thought to it before, thinking she was out of reach for both of them. But now, after he finally had her in his arms, he was on the verge of losing her again—and this time to a man who was like his brother.

He pulled her in close. "Baby, we both need more rest. Let me sleep on this, okay?"

"Okay. I really love you, Chance, and I don't want to lose you."

"I love you, too, sweetheart." He felt more of her tears fall on his chest, which crushed him. He wanted to say something that would make her feel better, but what could he say? Nothing.

Chapter Ten

Jaris put his arm around five-year-old Jake, who was the son of Belle, Shane, and Corey Blue.

"Mr. Jaris, the water is changed for all the dogs," Juan, Jake's brother, said.

"We also cleaned out the pens for Rex, Blue, King, and Rosie." Stephen was one of the older boys. "They'll be all set once they are found and come home."

The sadness in his voice was clear. All the boys were worried about the dogs. So was he. *So is Kaylyn.*

"Very good job." He was anxious to get finished with the chores and get to Kaylyn and Chance.

His talk with Emmett last night had turned him around. He was envisioning jumping into the Destiny way of life heart and soul.

* * * *

Kaylyn walked into the kitchen, glad to be on her feet again. But it was the only thing good about this morning. Last night, Chance's response to her confession about her feelings for Jaris devastated her. Why had she expected Chance to act differently? He wasn't from Destiny. He didn't understand. Jaris wasn't from Destiny either. Would he understand? *Probably not. Hell, I don't even know how he feels about me.*

Kaylyn closed her eyes, wondering if she should've kept quiet about her true feelings. Had she made a terrible mistake? She started trembling from head to toe.

Chance was in the shower.

I feel like a little girl who needs her mommy.

She knew her mom would be asleep given the time difference between Hawaii and Colorado. But her emotional need was taking over her common sense.

I really want to talk to her.

She got her cell and called her mom.

"Kaylyn, are you okay?" The panic in her mom's voice came through loud and clear.

"Physically, Mom, I couldn't be better." She choked back her tears. "But I'm in love and I'm falling apart."

"Kaylyn, I know Chance loves you."

"I know he does, too, but I'm not sure that's enough. Mom, I also love Jaris." She told her mother about what she'd said to Chance and how he'd reacted. "So you see, I may lose them both and I haven't even told Jaris how I feel about him."

"Sweetheart, love is a strong emotion, and you're a very smart girl. I know you will handle this just fine. You're not going to lose Chance. I promise you. He's loved you for a long time. After you talk to Jaris, the three of you need to sit down together and go through everything. That's what I had to do with your dads. You know they were only casual friends when we started dating. Talk about being scared I would lose them both...I know exactly how you feel. But you know what I told them? Get used to it. This is the way it's going to be. And you know, Kaylyn, we've been happy ever after."

"Oh, Mom, you make me feel so much better." She thought about her two dads, who worked hard in the oil fields of Alaska and were gone for months at a time. But when they came home, they always swept her mother up in their arms and disappeared for a couple days. When they emerged into the light of day, all three of them always had broad smiles. "I am going to tell them what you told my dads."

* * * *

Chance let the shower continue to run though he already cleaned and rinsed off. He was still wrestling with what Kaylyn had told him last night.

Even with the water running, he was able to hear a knock on the door, which brought him back to the present. *That's not Jaris's knock.*

* * * *

"Mom, Jaris is here. Wish me luck."

Another knock.

"Luck, baby. I love you."

"I love you, too."

* * * *

Chance threw on his robe, grabbed Annie's lead, and shot out the bathroom. He could hear Kaylyn walking to the front door. "Stop."

"What's the matter?" she asked him.

"That's not Jaris." He stepped right next to her. "Look out the peephole. Tell me who you see."

"I have no idea who that man is."

He pulled her behind him and reached for the sheriff's department handheld radio, which was on the table by the front door. Kaylyn's family home was a few miles out of town and at the end of a dirt road. There were only four houses on the street, each having several acres.

Kaylyn leaned in close to him. He could feel her trembling.

"Chance, I've seen a picture of Lunceford. That's not him outside."

"Doesn't matter who it is. We need to be careful." He pressed the button of the radio. "This is Chance Reynolds. There's a stranger at Kaylyn Anderson's front door. Can someone be here right away?"

Dylan Strange's voice came back, "Chance, we have a team about a quarter mile from you. They're on their way now."

Another knock on the door.

"Come with me, now." He put his arm around Kaylyn and took her to the bedroom. "Do you have a gun?"

"Yes. It's in the top drawer of my dresser."

"I don't think we'll need it, but I'll get it just in case."

* * * *

As his heart jackhammered in his chest, Jaris jumped in Emmett's truck with Sugar. Hearing Chance on the radio had filled him with dread.

He reached into his jacket and touched the handle of his pistol. The familiar talisman didn't work to calm his fears. Blind or not, if he and Emmett arrived and found someone had hurt Kaylyn or Chance, he would use his other senses to locate the bastard and empty every bullet in his gun into the fucker.

The roar of the engine told Jaris that Emmett was pushing his truck to the max. He felt the vehicle turn off the highway and onto the dirt road that led to Kaylyn's house.

"Jaris, I see the sheriff," Emmett informed him. "He's already here with several other officers. Kaylyn and Chance are fine. They're talking to Nicole on the porch."

He let out a breath of relief. "What about the stranger?"

"Jason is talking to the guy by the squad car." Emmett parked the truck. "Looks like this might've been a false alarm."

"We'll see." Jaris exited the cab with Sugar, heading the direction he could hear Kaylyn's voice. He had to be sure she was really okay.

"Oh, Jaris, you're never going to believe this." Kaylyn grabbed his hand and squeezed. "Mr. Bayless has four dogs that are already trained. They just need one week of our training. So we'll have dogs for our people. We won't have to delay a thing."

The exuberance in her voice was clear, but he wasn't convinced.

Sounds like too much of a coincidence to me. "How did this guy know you needed dogs?"

"He saw one of our postings on the school's Facebook page about our missing dogs." Her voice cracked, mentioning the four beloved canines. "Since Mr. Bayless is in the same field, he wanted to help."

"Help? Or did he want to get paid?"

She smiled. "Always a cop, aren't you. Yes. Of course he wants to be paid. You know how much it costs to train dogs. I'll gladly pay him. Jaris, I won't have to disappoint our clients. They will get their service dogs as scheduled."

"Hold on, Kaylyn. Not so fast." His police training kicked in. "We need to get his credentials checked out first."

"I agree," Chance said.

"So does the sheriff." Nicole was still one of the best officers Jaris had ever known. "I've already sent a message to Jena. The team over at TBK will run a complete background check on Mr. Bayless."

"Good. I'd like to talk to him myself."

"Actually, Jaris, the sheriff asked me to bring you to him once you arrived on scene. He says that you're the best interrogator he's ever seen. I have to agree."

"I appreciate that and definitely want to talk to this man." He turned to his best friend. "Chance, keep Kaylyn here."

"Sure thing."

"Jaris, I don't understand." Her excitement about the possibility of being able to have dogs for the four clients had vanished from her tone. "Do you think this really could somehow be connected to Kip Lunceford?"

"Until we know for sure that this guy is on the up and up, we have to be extra careful." There were so many other things he wanted to talk to Kaylyn about than this, but it couldn't be helped. This was what they all faced at the moment. Hopefully, it would all get resolved quickly and he could talk with her and Chance alone. "Sugar, let's go talk to this man."

Nicole led him over to Jason and the stranger. "Sheriff, here's Deputy Simmons as you requested."

"Thanks, Coleman. Mr. Bayless, this is one of my finest officers. I'm sure you won't mind answering a few questions from him."

"I don't mind at all." The man had a slight lisp, and his accent placed him from somewhere back East. Likely Boston or somewhere in Maine. "I'm very impressed you have a blind man on your force, Sheriff."

He didn't want to show all his cards. "Mr. Bayless, I'm more of a consultant."

Bayless shook his hand. "Whatever you are, it's impressive to me. My work with the blind and disabled gives me a unique perspective into your world, Deputy. I'm certain that those around you underestimate your abilities. Am I right?"

Jaris shrugged, believing the man was only trying to soften him up with compliments. "I can get around pretty well, thanks to Sugar."

"She's beautiful. One of Ms. Anderson's?"

"Yes. I understand you train service dogs, too. Tell me about that."

Mr. Bayless went into detail about his work. It was clear the man did have a great deal of knowledge about canines. Jaris didn't have to ask too many questions, as Bayless was a man who seemed to like to dominate conversations. Good thing. Made the job of an interrogator easier. But even listening to all Bayless said, he couldn't find a crack in his story. Was he telling the truth? Jaris's gut told him Bayless was holding something back.

"I have the dogs in the back of my van. Would you like to meet them, Deputy? I'm sure Ms. Anderson would."

"Ms. Anderson can meet them later, but I would like to meet your dogs now."

Chapter Eleven

Jaris walked into the sheriff's office with Sugar. He had a million questions but no answers so far. There were too many loose ends that needed to be tied up.

Potter had shot Kaylyn. He didn't buy his story one bit. The four dogs were still missing. Lunceford was still gunning for Belle. A stranger showed up at Kaylyn's door with an offer to give her four dogs. None of it was adding up. Were these things somehow connected? *I can't put my finger on it, but I'm sure they are.*

"Good. Everyone is here. Have a seat, Jaris," Sheriff Wolfe said. "I'm glad you convinced Kaylyn to stay at her house with Chance."

"And I'm glad you have Dylan and Nicole guarding her place. Who else is here?"

The sheriff informed him that Jena, Sean, and Matt were present. These three were quite the tech team. They knew hardware, software, and electronic tracking better than anyone. Sean and Matt were members of Shannon's Elite and had been with the CIA for several years already. Jena, their new wife and former hacker, also was a member of the Agency's local team.

Jaris was ready to get down to business. "Tell me what you have so far on Bayless."

"He's seems to be cooperating fully," Jason said. "The man has handed over all his identification and given us all his credentials."

"So far we haven't found anything in Bayless's records that seems out of the ordinary." Jena's voice was similar in some ways to Kaylyn's, reminding him he needed to get through this briefing and back to her and Chance. There was a lot he wanted to tell them.

"I'll give the okay to Kaylyn about taking Bayless up on his offer. He can bring his dogs to the Boys Ranch. Lyle can make sure his dogs get the rest of Kaylyn's training and are ready for their new owners. Chance and I will stay close to Kaylyn."

"I'll keep tabs on Bayless to make sure he doesn't have some other agenda," Jason said.

"Good idea, Sheriff." Jaris was glad this man wore a badge. Destiny was in good hands. He turned his attention to Jena, Sean, and Matt. "Please keep digging into Bayless's records."

"We will," Sean said. "Don't worry about that."

"What about Potter and his four supposed physician friends? Anything on that front?"

"No," Matt answered. "Like Bayless's records, all nice and clean."

Jaris felt Sugar shift at his feet. He patted her on the head. She always could tell when something was bothering him. "I just don't have a good feeling about any of it, Sheriff."

"Neither do I, but I need something to go on before I can make any arrests."

"I understand. What about Lunceford and his sister?"

"All is quiet."

"Too quiet," Jaris said.

"Yep, but Dragon Week seems to be going off without a hitch. I've got at least fifteen officers on duty at any time. Shane and Corey are with Belle wherever she goes. She's safe. I'm glad you and Chance are keeping an eye on Kaylyn. I've assigned two officers to watch her neighborhood. They won't be more than five minutes away at any time."

"Are Potter and his buddies still in town?" Jena asked.

"Yes, they are," the sheriff answered. "So are their two slimeball attorneys."

An idea occurred to Jaris. "Jena, have you three checked the credentials of the lawyers?"

"No, but that's something we'll get right on."

"You might be on to something, Jaris," Sean said. "Thanks for the suggestion."

"That's all for now," the sheriff said. "If you three turn up anything, let me know and I'll get everyone together for another briefing."

Jaris heard the trio stand.

"We definitely will," Sean said.

"Jaris, I heard you did some fine detective work yourself the past few days," Matt said. "Glad to have you on the team."

"Thanks. Glad to be here." Jaris meant it. There was no place like Destiny. He might've only been here for a short time, but he already felt like it was home. These were his friends. He wanted to keep all of the citizens safe, but especially Kaylyn.

He stood.

"Jaris, do you mind sticking around for a moment," the sheriff said.

"Not at all." He sat back down, wondering what Jason wanted to talk to him about.

"We'll see you guys later," Jena said. "Jaris, thanks for the suggestion."

"I hope it helps you."

"We'll find the link between these assholes to Lunceford. I know there has to be one."

After the three left, he leaned forward in the chair. "What's up, Sheriff?"

"As you know, quite a bit is up. Our town is at war and we need men like you on our side."

Our town. He liked that the sheriff saw him as a part of Destiny. "I am ready to do whatever you need."

"That's good to hear. I deputized you and Chance along with a lot of other people just for Dragon Week. With all the outsiders attending the festival, I needed to bolster the numbers on my team."

"Like I told you before, I'm happy to serve."

"And your service has been amazing. I've never known anyone with better interrogation skills than you. I need you beyond Dragon Week, Jaris. You and Nicole were once partners. Like you, her law enforcement skills are incredible. Having her as my deputy has been one of the best things to happen during my career. Nicole respects you. I respect you. And the whole town sees you as a hero."

"I'm hardly a hero."

"Humble, too. You're exactly what I need. I'd like to make you a permanent member of my team. What do you say?"

After losing his sight, Jaris had never let himself dream he would be able to return to law enforcement. He'd accepted his fate. But in Destiny, fate sometimes smiled on you in ways you never imagined. "Damn, Sheriff. What a surprise."

"Surprise or not, I want you. Can I count on you?"

"If I can be of service to you and this town, I would love to be part of your team."

* * * *

Kaylyn adjusted the mike stand to her height.

Off to her left, Patrick O'Leary was taking questions from the audience. The Q&A would last for another couple of minutes, and then Wolfe Mayhem was scheduled to play.

Godric came up and handed her a bottle of water. "Good to see you on your feet, love."

"It feels good, too. Thanks." Out of the corner of her eye, she spied Chance standing next to the stage with Annie by his side. How could she make him understand? His reaction to her confession that she also had feelings for Jaris had been painful to witness.

Godric strapped on his bass. "Still hurts?"

He's talking about my leg and not my heart. "A little, but not too bad." She took a sip of water. "I appreciate this."

Big Jim pulled a stool close to her. "Just in case you need to sit. It won't hurt a thing if you do."

"You guys are treating me like a princess." She laughed. "I kind of like it."

"You've got the best pipes I've ever heard." Hank gave her the set list. "Whether you sit or stand…it won't make any difference in how wonderful you'll sing tonight."

She smiled. "Thanks. That's very thoughtful of all of you. Where's Mitchell?"

"Where do you think?" Godric grinned. "He's with Phoebe, the love of his and his two brothers' lives. The passion between those four is something else, isn't it?"

She nodded. "Phoebe is a very lucky woman."

Glancing over the heads of the audience to the northeast corner of the park at The Red Dragon statue, one of the four dragon statues that surrounded the green space, she stared directly into the eyes of the beast. The Red Dragon, though most locals called it The Passion Dragon, had the image of a heart embedded on its chest.

She nodded. *Passion? That's what has gotten me into trouble these past couple of days…and nights. You bad dragon.*

There was no sign of Jaris. He likely was still at the sheriff's office checking on Mr. Bayless. Both Jaris and Chance were quite protective of her and suspicious of strangers. Bayless's offer, if valid, would sure make things easier for her. With Doc's orders that she couldn't help train dogs for a while longer and with her four dogs missing, she really needed Bayless to be legit. She had four clients who were coming in the next few days to start their weeklong training with their new companions.

Mitchell walked up onstage. "I heard about your unexpected visitor today, Kaylyn."

"Jason told you? What else did your brother tell you?"

"He hasn't told me anything. I heard about it from our fiancée."

"Ah." Kaylyn was so glad that Phoebe had finally returned to the loving arms of the three Wolfe brothers. Those four belonged together. "Seems like everyone in town is keeping an eye on Bayless. I know we're all on edge because of Lunceford, but Mr. Bayless might actually be a good guy who just wants to help me."

"Maybe." Mitchell took a seat behind his drums. He pointed at the back of the stage with one of his sticks, where Jaris was coming up the stairs with Sugar. "I bet we're about to find out about Bayless's credentials."

Jaris walked over to her. "How are you doing, Kaylyn?"

"I'll be better when our dogs are found." She needed to talk to him, but here and now was not the place. Later. She wasn't going to let anything stop her tonight. "What did you find out about Bayless? Can we take him up on his offer?"

"For now. Yes." Jaris's tone was clear. He still didn't trust the man.

"That's great news. Did you call Lyle and let him know?"

"I did. The sheriff is going to take Bayless and his dogs up to the Boys Ranch tonight. Emmett is going to put Bayless up in a RV at the ranch for the time being."

"I'm so happy we won't have to disappoint our four clients."

"We'll see. I still want Lyle to check out his dogs, and Chance and I to run them through your tests."

"I agree." She wanted to make sure the new dogs were up to her standards. "You better go stand with Chance. The band's part of the show is about to start."

He grabbed her hand and squeezed, sending a spark up her arm. "You're going to blow them away, Kaylyn."

"I'll do my best." She felt her heart skip a couple of beats as Jaris stepped back to where Chance was standing.

Patrick continued answering questions. "Absolutely there are dragons in Oklahoma. I have a report from one of our supporters who saw a baby purple dragon outside of Norman flying in the sky. Which reminds me, be sure to visit our website. You'll find all kinds of testimonial sightings from people all around the world." Patrick looked at his watch. "I see my time is almost up. I know you are anxious to hear Wolfe Mayhem perform. I can only take one more question."

Someone from the crowd spoke up. "I don't have a question but I would like to make a comment, Mr. O'Leary."

Kaylyn recognized the voice and felt her breath catch in her throat. *Potter.*

She looked up and saw her shooter standing in the back. The words to signal Chance and Jaris were sitting on her lips. *I see a cowboy out there.* But she kept quiet, seeing several Destonians surrounding Dr. Potter, who were ready to take him down if necessary.

"I would like to apologize to you and to this whole town. But there is one woman who I need to ask forgiveness of more than anyone else." Potter's eyes fixed on hers.

Holding on to her mike, she felt weak in the knees and sat back down on the stool that Big Jim had placed behind her. In a flash, Chance and Jaris were up onstage and moving right in front of her, using their own bodies as cover.

"Miss Anderson, I am truly sorry for what happened to you. I didn't mean to shoot you and I hope you'll forgive me. It was just an accident."

Clicking off the power switch to the mike, she reached out and touched Chance and Jaris. "Guys, it's okay. He's not going to do anything here. Not with all of Jason's deputies on duty."

They didn't budge. *God, they can be so stubborn.*

Mitchell left his drums and came up behind her. "We need to get you offstage, Kaylyn."

"No, Mitchell. Let me handle this." She clicked the power switch on. "Mr. Potter, I appreciate your apology."

"You can't imagine how glad I am to hear that." Potter sounded so different than he had when Jaris had been interrogating him. His tone was contrite. Was it only an act?

She stood and moved to the side of Chance, allowing her a glimpse of her shooter.

"Potter has at least eight of Jason's deputies all around him," she whispered to Jaris and Chance. "Please. I'm safe. I have a show to do."

"Ms. Anderson, I would like to pay for all your medical bills."

"I have insurance, Mr. Potter."

"But I'm the one at fault. You shouldn't have to pay a dime and neither should your insurance."

"Listen to him, guys," Kaylyn whispered. "Even if he's lying, it's clear he won't try anything here. I'm supposed to sing."

Chance turned around and faced her. "Here's the deal. Jaris and I will remain beside you onstage with Sugar and Annie through the whole set."

Jaris nodded. "And once the band is finished, Chance and I will take you home."

"Okay."

Chance added, "There will be no meet-and-greet for you to talk to the band's fans. Understand?"

"Seriously? That's part of the job."

"Listen to your men, Kaylyn," Mitchell said. "Either we do it their way or I pull the plug on tonight's performance. The guys and I can sign all the autographs. It will be fine."

"Please, Ms. Anderson," Potter's voice sounded desperate. "Let me do this for you."

Chance took the mike from her. "Mr. Potter, this is not the time or the place to talk about this."

Jaris leaned into the microphone. "Potter, you've said enough. You need to leave. Now."

The man nodded and left the row of seats. Seeing how strong and commanding Chance and Jaris were being, she knew they could be perfect Doms—*for her.*

"He left like you asked," she told them. "Jacob is following him. Trouble averted."

Chance handed the mike back to her. "What's it going to be, sweetheart? Are you going to do it our way and do the set and leave, or are we going to take you off this stage right now?"

"We'll do it your way. I'll sing. When the show ends, we can go back to my place."

Mitchell sat back down by his drums.

Patrick cleared his throat. "Please put your hands together and welcome Wolfe Mayhem."

The crowd roared.

Glad to have Chance and Jaris so close, Kaylyn brought the mike to her mouth and sang the opening number, though her thoughts were on what was going to happen after the show.

Having Chance and Jaris together at her home would give her the opportunity to talk with both of them about how she felt. Was her mother right? Should she be blunt about what she really wanted? Would it change everything?

Chapter Twelve

Though Chance would've loved just listening to Kaylyn sing, he knew he must focus all his senses on everything happening around her. Kaylyn's safety depended on it.

Doing the same thing as he was, Jaris stood on the other side of the stage next to her.

The band transitioned into another upbeat song, making it difficult to hear. But Chance still had his other senses to pull from, and the vibration he felt through his boots told him someone other than a band member was coming up on the stage from behind.

Chance tugged on Annie's lead, letting her know to be on guard. Her wagging tail indicated she knew the person approaching. Knowing this was a friend and not a foe allowed his shoulders to relax, though he remained on guard.

"It's me, buddy."

He instantly recognized Emmett's voice, even though his words were nearly being drowned out by Wolfe Mayhem's music.

Almost having to shout to be heard, Chance asked, "Everything okay?"

"So far, but after hearing that creep talk, everyone is on alert. Come over to the side behind the speakers for a moment. I need to talk to you about Kaylyn."

Taking a few steps to the side with Emmett, he asked, "What about her?"

"I wanted you to know that me and my brothers will help Lyle take care of everything up at the Boys Ranch until Potter is either behind bars or out of town. Don't worry about a thing. I realize that all your focus is on Kaylyn, exactly where it should be, especially after we all heard Potter's outburst."

"Thanks, Emmett. No matter what, I'm going to make sure she's safe. I have no doubt that Jaris is on the same page as me."

"I'm sure you're right about that. Before coming up onstage, I talked to the sheriff. He's adding two more deputies to the detail keeping an eye on her house."

"Perfect, because this would be an opportune time to break into her home since everyone is in town celebrating Dragon Week." Chance heard Kaylyn begin singing a ballad about a woman who lost her one chance at love, which reminded him of her admission of her deep feelings for Jaris. *This isn't the time to think about that. Keeping her safe is all that matters now.* "Once the band is finished with their set, Jaris and I want to get her back to her house."

Emmett placed his hand on his shoulder. "I'll drive the three of you. I'm going to pull my truck up behind the stage so that we can make a fast exit."

"I appreciate all you're doing for Kaylyn and for me and Jaris."

"Buddy, that's what friends are for." Emmett exited the stage.

Without hesitation, Chance moved back to the position he'd just left, right next to Kaylyn.

* * * *

"Thanks for the ride, Emmett." Standing on her sidewalk, Kaylyn got her keys out of her purse.

"You're very welcome."

Chance stood to her left with Annie. Jaris had gone with Sugar across the dirt road in front of Mrs. Nevelson's house. He was talking to Dylan and the other officers who had been patrolling the neighborhood.

"Great show tonight." Emmett turned to Chance. "You and Jaris take care of her, and call me if you need anything."

"We have your number. We will call you at the first sign of anything out of the ordinary."

"Good deal." Emmett got back into his truck and drove off.

Jaris headed to her house from across the street. "The sheriff has done an incredible job securing the area. We shouldn't have any issues tonight."

Finally. Alone with Jaris and Chance.

She placed the key in the deadbolt and unlocked the door. "Have a seat, guys. I could use a glass of wine. Would you two like anything?"

"You've been on your injured leg too long," Jaris said. "You sit and Chance and I can get the drinks and something to eat. I bet you're hungry?"

"Not really." Food was the last thing on her mind.

"Sweetheart, you sure? You haven't eaten all day." Chance's tone sent a shiver up and down her spine. Like always, it was filled with a deep, abiding kindness, but there was a hint of sadness she detected that caused her to choke up.

"You and Jaris haven't eaten either."

"How about we start with some cheese and crackers? Or would you rather Jaris cook something?"

"Cheese and crackers will be fine. Thank you both."

They walked into her kitchen and she sat down on her sofa. Her heart was racing. She'd been waiting for what seemed like forever, though it had only been since last night, to tell Jaris how she really felt about him. *How do I tell him? How will he react?* She'd already experienced Chance's reaction to her truth. Not good, though she hadn't given up hope yet.

She brought out her cell and sent a text to her mother. "*Getting cold feet, Mom. Alone with them now. What do I do?*"

Waiting for her mother's response, she listened to Jaris and Chance preparing their light meal.

Her cell beeped.

She read her mother's words and felt better.

"Dreams are never reached unless you do everything you can to reach them, honey. I say, 'Go for it.' Love, Mom."

Bolstered by her mother's text, she smiled and put her phone back in her purse.

The guys returned with the food and drink.

She took the glass of wine Jaris held out for her.

Chance placed the tray on the coffee table.

She scooted to the center of her couch. "Guys, sit down with me." They squeezed next to her. It felt so good being between them. "I have something I've been wanting to say all day."

Jaris placed his glass on the table and turned to her. "I have something I need to say, too."

"Please, Jaris. Let me go first." Even though she was determined to follow through with this, she began to tremble.

He grabbed her hand. "Sure."

"It's just that…well, I need to tell you…" She took a deep breath and blurted, "Oh, damn it. I am in love with you, Jaris."

"Oh my God, Kaylyn. That's what I wanted to tell you. I'm in love with you, too."

Happy tears welled up in her eyes. She leaned forward and pressed her lips to his. Feeling him deepen the kiss, tingles spread all over her body.

She tried to kiss the other man of her dreams, but he turned his head away. Her heart seemed to seize in her chest. "Chance, please. You have to understand this doesn't change how I feel about you. I've loved you for years, and that will never change. But my heart is big enough to love Jaris, too."

"Sweetheart, I want to make you happy, but I don't know if I can do this." Chance grabbed her hand. "Kaylyn, I'm sorry, but honestly this is so strange to me."

Jaris bristled. "What the hell, Chance? This is Destiny. This is how Kaylyn grew up."

"I love this town and I love her, but I didn't grow up this way."

She squeezed Chance's hand. "But can't you just try?"

"I'm not sure."

She'd known him for years. He was decisive about everything. This was so unlike Chance. It was ripping her heart apart. Her mind swirled with a million things to say to try to convince him it would work—for all of them. She was terrified she was going to lose him again, and this time it would be forever. *I just can't let that happen. What can I do?*

Needing a moment to collect her thoughts and not wanting to break down in front of them, she stood. "I'll be back, guys."

* * * *

Jaris sat in silence, hearing Kaylyn shut the bathroom door. When he heard the water running, he said, "You're breaking her heart, Chance. You know that, right?"

"How can you accept this? You're not from here either."

As much as he hated listening to the pain in Chance's voice, he now knew what Kaylyn wanted, needed. "Because I love Kaylyn and will do anything for her, that's how. And I know you do to."

"I don't know what to say, Jaris. I do love her. With all my heart but I'm just not wired that way. It felt so weird when you two kissed just now."

"Of course it's weird. This is new for both of us." Jaris needed to turn him around and fast. They were about to lose the woman of both their dreams. "You're like a brother to me, Chance. I never had any siblings. My dad is gone. You're the only family I have."

Chance placed his hand on his shoulder "You're a brother to me too, Jaris. But is that enough?"

"I believe it can be. Sharing Kaylyn with you would give me the family I don't have anymore."

"Sounds so simple, but this kind of thing only works out in movies and books for people like us." Chance's tone made it clear he was wrestling with the whole idea and not coming up with any answers. "If I'd been born here, grew up in a family like hers, known this my whole life…it would be so easy. But I'm from a family with one dad and one mom. I have a sister. We're the typical family that exists everywhere outside of this town."

"And how was your life before you came to Destiny?"

"Nothing was wrong with my life. My parents are great. I love them both. My sister, Paige and I have always been close."

"I'm not talking about your family, Chance. I'm talking about you and Kaylyn. It didn't take me any time to realize that you two belong together. How long did you both keep your feelings buried? I know you came to Destiny to be closer to her, not just to help her train dogs."

Chance sighed. "For years.

"Wasted years. You taught me how to *see* again and also that blindness comes in all kinds of shades." He hoped he was getting through to him. "Remember?"

"Yes. It's one of the first things I say to my students. So?"

"I'll never forget your words, Chance. 'Even the seeing are blind to so much that is right in front of them.'"

"What does that have to do with this?"

"Don't be blind to how much she loves you. I have no doubt this won't be easy for either of us at first, but we will figure it out—for her."

* * * *

Kaylyn turned off the faucet and stepped into the tub. While filling it, she'd heard bits and pieces of Chance and Jaris's conversation, which was still going on.

God, men can be so hardheaded sometimes.

She'd left them in the living room, needing a moment to clear her head, and nothing cleared her head better than a hot bath.

Submerged in the steamy water, a few tears fell.

But tears never solved anything.

As she quickly washed her body, she decided it was past time for action.

They'd both declared their love for her. *It's their dream, too. They just don't know it.*

She could hear Jaris still working on convincing a stubborn Chance to consider giving the Destiny way of life a try, but even Jaris had expressed that he thought it would be difficult.

Difficult? God, she would never understand how being in love could be so hard. Why did the outside world put such limits on it?

Limits? "No more. I'm getting what I want."

She stepped out of the tub and reached for a towel, determined to have her dream. Or in her case, *dreams.* Chance and Jaris were sitting on her sofa in her house at this very moment.

She dropped the towel to the floor, leaving her bathrobe on the hook. "Get ready, guys. Kaylyn is in the house." She turned the knob and smiled. "She knows what she wants and is willing to do what she has to do to get it."

Without hesitation, she walked into the hall to the men who had stolen her heart.

Chapter Thirteen

Chance heard Kaylyn walking out of the bathroom back to the living room, where he and Jaris still remained.

While she had been bathing, the discussion with Jaris had gone in circles. Yes, he wanted Kaylyn. So did Jaris. She wanted both of them. Jaris was willing to try, but he still wasn't sure. Over and over he and Jaris had talked through it, from every conceivable direction, but coming to no real resolution. He'd been honest with Jaris, voicing just a few of the difficulties sharing Kaylyn would have. Jaris had countered all his arguments with all the reasons why such a relationship might work.

Might? That was what held Chance up and clearly was also in the back of Jaris's mind, even if he didn't say so. If it didn't work, then what? Disaster, that was what.

Kaylyn's footsteps came to a stop on the other side of her coffee table, opposite him and Jaris. "I've been listening to all your discussion, and since it's about me, I think it's my turn to put my two cents' worth in."

"Sweetheart, you know I love you but—"

"Chance, I'm tired of *buts.*"

"Kaylyn, don't be angry with him. It's a lot for all of us to digest." Jaris was obviously struggling with the idea of sharing her as much as he was. "We just need to talk this out."

"No. It's time for you both to listen to me."

Chance was familiar with her putting her foot down. "Okay, sweetheart. You have the floor."

"I think we've established that we all love each other. You both are like brothers. I heard a lot of *what ifs*. There are no guarantees to any relationship, but when there is love, you definitely have a head start on it lasting forever. Look at all the wonderful examples we have on how to make it work. My parents. The O'Learys. And so many more. Observing them, I've learned one of the main things people need to make a family last is to talk to one another. Just like we're doing now. Because there will be trials. That's life. But if you have love, communication, and commitment, you can work out anything. I know this isn't the life that either of you ever imagined. But it's the life I always dreamed of. It can work. We can make it work. I love you both. And I want you both, too. And I believe you both want me."

"Yes. I want you," Jaris said.

Her words shook Chance to his core. "Baby, of course I want you."

He heard her step around the coffee table, and sit down between them on the sofa. Her freshly cleaned skin's aroma filled his nostrils.

She grabbed his hand and Jaris's hand. "I'm right here, ready to be yours."

She brought his hand up to her naked breast, which ignited his hunger for her. He could tell that Jaris was massaging her other breast.

"No clothes? You don't play fair, do you, baby?" Jaris's voice rumbled at a deep, hungry tone.

"She never has," Chance answered for her, moving his fingers lightly over her soft flesh. His unrestrained lust was pushing him forward, despite his reservations. He had to have her. Now.

"And neither do you play fair, Mr. Reynolds. As long as I get what I want, I'll let you win." She was making it clear what she wanted.

He leaned over and kissed her, tracing her lips with his tongue. "I really want to try, sweetheart."

She brought her delicate fingers up to his face. "That's all I'm asking, Chance. For you to try. I know this will work. For you. For Jaris. For me. For all of us." She pressed her lips back to his again.

When she turned and kissed Jaris, he still felt strange and awkward, but somehow now it was lesser than before. *Maybe this really can work. Maybe she's right.*

Wanting to give her what she desired, Chance shoved down his hesitation, running his hand up and down her arm. He could hear Jaris and Kaylyn's kiss deepen. *Oh my God, can I really do this? Yes, I can.*

He took a deep breath and moved his lips over her breast, suckling on her sweet nipple. The kissing sounds ended, and Jaris shifted down. Suddenly, he felt Jaris's head bump hard into his head. The loud thud reverberated throughout the room.

"Guess I was caught up in the moment and forgot about you, buddy. Sorry about that." Jaris started laughing.

Jaris's laughter was contagious, and Chance began to join in.

"What are you two laughing about? How hard did you hit each other's head? Are you both okay?" Kaylyn's voice of concern was one of the sweetest sounds he'd ever heard. She was truly an angel on earth.

Catching his breath from all the hysterics, Chance kissed her little soft nipple. "I'm fine."

"Me too, baby."

The collision and laughter had relaxed him just right. His doubts crawled down deep into his core. Reluctance vanished. All he could think of was how much he wanted to pleasure Kaylyn. Keeping one of his hands on her breast, he ran the other one down her body, bumping into Jaris, doing the same.

"This is kind of awkward on this sofa," Jaris said. "Let's take our girl back into the bedroom where we can have more room."

Our girl? It sounded odd to him. "Agreed." Deciding to tease Kaylyn, he said, "Come on, Annie. Come on, girl."

"You're a devil, Mr. Reynolds." Kaylyn's voice was full of mock rage. She clearly knew he was kidding.

"I am, but I meant you, sweetheart." He lifted her up into his arms, following Jaris back to her bedroom. Gently, he lowered her down to the bed. He and Jaris ordered Annie and Sugar to lie down on the floor.

"I'm naked." Kaylyn giggled. "Isn't it past time you two were, too?"

He smiled. "I thought women were more about touch than the visuals, sweetheart."

"I guarantee you that I'll be able to touch you better without all those clothes." She ran her fingers down his jawline. "What do you say?"

"I say 'yes.' Hell yes." Jaris began undressing.

As odd as this moment was, Chance stepped off the bed. "You don't have to ask me twice."

His only thought swirling in his head was to please her. "Jaris, why don't we give *our girl* a strip show?" Calling her *our girl* still felt odd on his lips. Would he ever get used to it?

"Great idea, buddy." Jaris stepped back. "Slow and easy. Make her drool for us."

"Both of you are wicked." The light tone in her voice told him she was enjoying this.

Chance brought his hands up to his shirt and began to unbutton it slowly, moving his body in the sexiest dance move he knew.

"Very nice. Take it off, baby. Yes. A little music might help you two out." Kaylyn shifted on the bed, and music filled the room.

He didn't recognize the song, but the beat was deep and vibrated over his skin. He undid the last button of his shirt, and parted it, revealing his chest for her eyes.

"Oh my God, you both are so beautiful." The wantonness in her voice spurred him on more.

He removed his shirt, holding it in his hand. "You like?"

"Oh yes, I like. I like very much."

"And this?" Jaris asked, obviously referring to his own body.

In a breathy tone, she answered, "So much. Give me more."

Chance lifted his shirt and twirled it above his head. "More to come, sweetheart. More to come." He tossed it to the floor, and began unbuttoning his 501s. His balls got heavy and his cock came to attention.

"My God, you both are so big."

"Are you talking about our muscles or something else, sweetheart?" He loved teasing her, always had.

She giggled. "Both. You can't imagine how much you look alike."

Jaris snorted. "If you're talking about our cocks, I don't really care to find out, baby. You know how we *see.*"

"I'm in complete agreement with him, sweetheart. I don't want to touch his junk. Ever."

Kaylyn went into hysterics, which got his engine running even more. Odd, but true. "I'll tell you this, they are probably the largest on the planet. If you ever wanted to pose for *Playgirl*, I'm sure they would be more than happy to give both of you the centerfold."

The levity was somehow lifting the awkwardness of all of this. He grinned, jumping into the spirit of the moment. "And I'm betting *Playboy* would make you playmate of the year. Won't the publishers be surprised when two blind men buy out all the issues."

All three of them laughed.

"I loved the show. Your bodies are absolute male perfection. So beautiful."

"Time to wrap this beauty up with a condom." Jaris ripped a foil package. "You have protection, Chance?"

"Yes." He knelt down and reached in the pocket of his jeans, which were on the floor. He pulled out the condom he'd taken from the box in Kaylyn's nightstand their first night together.

"Won't you two join me on the bed? I'm getting cold."

"I believe I know how to warm you up, baby," Jaris said.

"Me too, buddy. Me too."

* * * *

Having the bodies of the two men of her dreams next to her, Kaylyn's skin tingled as her temperature rose.

"Kaylyn, face Chance," Jaris ordered, sounding like a fully trained Dom.

She obeyed instantly, turning on her side. She was certain Jaris wanted her in this position, her front to Chance and her back to him, to try to help Chance become more comfortable. Of the two of them, Chance had been the most hesitant at the idea of sharing her.

She touched Chance on his full lips. He parted them, and brought his mouth to hers. Her toes curled as his kiss intensified.

Jaris traced her entire back with his fingers, *seeing* her with his touch. "God, she is so beautiful. Don't you agree, brother?"

"I certainly do." Chance kissed her on the neck, causing gooseflesh to rise over her body. He touched her breasts, moving his hand down to her pussy.

Jaris kissed the small of her back and gently massaged her ass.

Having their four hands and two mouths on her body caused the pressure inside her to grow and grow. It was maddening.

Chance sucked on her nipples until they became taut and ached. He threaded his fingers through her pussy, which dampened at his touch. Her clit began to throb.

Jaris fingered her anus, continuing his sensuous massage of her back.

This was where she belonged. With them. With her two men. She vibrated with passion and heat because of their intimate kisses and touches. Surrendering to them was as natural as breathing to her.

Chance pressed on her clit with his finger, sending an electric line through her body.

"Please. I need you inside me." It was the truth. Every syllable of it. Need permeated the cells of her body.

"Not yet, sweetheart." Chance was on the edge of his own desire.

Hoping to tempt him, she shifted her hips forward until her pussy was pressed against his monstrous cock.

"No you don't, Kaylyn." Chance's lips thinned, but somehow he kept his lust in check. How? His willpower amazed her.

When he pressed on her clit again, she nearly lost her mind. She'd never felt such need in her entire life. "Please. Oh please. I can't stand much more."

"Don't give in to her, Chance. She can take much more and should. If we hold back a little longer, the pleasure will blow her mind. Let her know who is in charge." Jaris gave her a love bite on her ass. Then he swiped his tongue between her cheeks, making her tremble. "Tell her, buddy. She's ours. All ours. Our little plaything."

Hearing Jaris's dominating tone made her tremble from head to toe. He was even more than she'd ever dreamed of.

Chance cupped her chin. "Just a little more, sweetheart. You can take it, can't you?"

"Yes," she whispered. "I can take it."

"Good, because I want to taste your juices. Your scent is driving me crazy." He shifted down the bed until his head was between her legs. She could feel the heat of his breath skating over her swollen folds. "God, you smell good."

Her heart was racing fast in her chest. She writhed between them, knowing she would soon have both their mouths on her body— Chance's on her pussy and Jaris's on her ass.

"You taste so sweet, Kaylyn. Like honey." Chance held her by the thighs and continued lapping up her juices.

Jaris circled her anus with his wicked tongue. Their dual oral torture added another layer to her already rising pressure.

Chance captured her clit between his lips, tightening just right on the tiny little bud.

"Yes. God. Yes." The pressure exploded into a million shivering sensations throughout her body. She bucked back and forth into each of their hungry mouths. The intensity of her orgasm shocked her, as mini dizzying explosions kept erupting inside her.

"I'm going first." Chance pulled her close to him, rolling her on her back and covering her body with his massive muscled frame.

Gazing into his handsome face, she thought about telling him they both could go first. She'd never had anal sex before, but was sure she would love it with them. But still shaking from her orgasm, she couldn't bring herself to suggest anything. They were in control. They were in charge. She was their *plaything,* as Jaris had called her. Just how she saw herself.

Jaris grabbed her wrists, pulling them above her head. "She's ours, Chance. All ours."

Chance kissed her and then thrust his cock into her pussy. His shaft stretched her insides and rubbed against that spot that gave her such immense pleasure.

In and out, he sent his cock, every one of his strokes creating delicious tremors through her body.

"God, you are so tight, sweetheart." Chance's words were hot and heavy. "You feel so good."

His thrusts continued slamming into her body, sending her higher and higher.

While kissing the palms of her hands, Jaris continued to hold her by the wrist.

"Going to come." Chance sent his cock deep into her pussy and held it there.

Being pierced so utterly by him, she gasped, feeling his body stiffen against her trembling flesh.

Her pussy began to spasm, clenching and unclenching and clenching again on his thick shaft.

As he came, Chance groaned like a lion. She came again, and every nerve sparked even hotter than before.

He and Jaris fumbled for a split second, changing places. Even in their moment of awkwardness, she felt their dominance over her.

Jaris was now on top of her, sending his cock into her pussy. "I've waited so long for you, Kaylyn. You're everything I imagined you would be and more."

His thrusts deepened, scraping the same spot that Chance had. Again, her desires multiplied. She wanted more. Needed more.

"Yes. Oh God. Yes."

"Come for us, baby." Jaris kissed her trembling lips. "One more time."

His thrusts came faster and harder.

She screamed as another climatic wave rolled through her body.

"Fuuuck." Jaris came inside her and then he collapsed on top of her.

He rolled to his side, pulling her with him. Chance came up behind her, now in the place Jaris had been in earlier.

"I love you, Kaylyn." Chance's words thrilled her.

Jaris touched her cheek. "And I love you, too."

"I love you both so very much." She wrapped her right arm around Jaris's neck and reached back and grabbed Chance's hand. "I will always love you."

Chapter Fourteen

Kaylyn yawned and stretched her arms over her head. The morning sun peeked through her blinds, illuminating her bedroom in a soft, warm glow. Jaris was asleep beside her. She could see Sugar on the floor next to his side of the bed. She rolled over, thinking she would find Chance. But he and Annie were gone. Chance wasn't a person to sleep in.

She swung her legs off the bed and tiptoed out of the bedroom to the bathroom. She could smell coffee, which told her Chance had made a pot. *Perfect. Just what I need to get the day started.*

She brushed her teeth and put on her robe, which she had left in there last night. She grinned at her image in the mirror. "You're a bit of a devil yourself, Miss Anderson, but your plan did work. Good for you."

She headed into the kitchen and found the coffee but no Chance. Where was he? *I bet he's checking with Jason's deputies about what, if anything, happened last night.*

She poured herself a cup of black coffee and sat down at her kitchen table. She reached for the morning paper. *Chance must've left it for me.*

Most of the articles were about Dragon Week. The review of Wolfe Mayhem's performance lifted her spirits.

"Wolfe Mayhem's songs knocked the socks off of the attendees of Dragon Week. They never disappoint their fans. The vocals of Miss Kaylyn Anderson, the band's lead singer, reach into your very soul, stirring all your emotions. Destiny's local band has put out their

second single, which is being played at radio stations all around Colorado and surrounding states. We are so privileged to have these talented musicians from our town."

There was a mention about her missing dogs in another section that made her eyes well up. She was afraid the worst might've happened. Still no sign of them.

The article went on to talk about Mr. Bayless offering his four dogs to her. Keeping anything under wraps in Destiny was impossible. She took a deep breath. Even if she had to follow Doc's rules about not training dogs, she still wanted Chance and Jaris to work with Bayless. Until her guys gave the green light, she wouldn't hand Bayless's dogs over to her clients.

On the inner page was a quick mention about Potter's outburst last night at the performance. She closed the paper, wondering if the man was truly sorry for shooting her.

After she'd finished her first cup and started on her second, Chance walked back into her house with Annie.

"Where have you been at this hour, Mr. Reynolds?"

"Talking with Dylan. How did you sleep, Miss Anderson?"

His tone seemed odd to her. Had Dylan told Chance something that had troubled him? "I slept great. How about you?"

"Fine. I need to get to the Boys Ranch. Lyle could use some help. Jaris put in his time. Now, it's my turn. It's not fair to the Stones for us to shirk our duties."

"Let's have a cup of coffee first. Then I'll get ready and take you."

"No. Dylan has agreed to drive me, sweetheart. You have another performance you need to rest up for. I'll be there with Jaris just like yesterday. Onstage. By your side."

"Will you at least have a cup of coffee with me?"

"No. Dylan is waiting. I have to go." He moved close to her and kissed her on the forehead. "Bye, Kaylyn."

Before she could say a word, he walked out of her house. *Something is definitely off with him.*

* * * *

"Do you care if I roll down my window?" Chance asked Dylan, who was driving him to the ranch.

"Not at all." The former Navy SEAL was now the current head of security of TBK as well as one of the team members of Shannon's Elite. "The air is brisk. Helps a man to clear his head. What's on your mind, Chance?"

The guy was intuitive for sure. "Not a 'what' but a 'who.' Kaylyn is on my mind."

"Just what I thought." Dylan drove over Silver Spoon Bridge.

"How could you possibly read me so well?"

"Years of training at Langley and good instincts."

Chance admired Dylan's no-nonsense demeanor. Who better to ask advice from than him? "Can you shed some light on how things work in Destiny?"

"Meaning?"

"You know…how do you and Cam…make things…hell, I don't know how to say this."

"How do we make it work with Erica?"

Straight to the point. God, I like this guy. "As a matter of fact, yes. I'm interested in knowing how you three do it."

"So Jaris finally got off the fence and let Kaylyn know he loved her, too? Didn't take him as long as you."

"Does the whole town know?"

Dylan laughed. "Of course. It was obvious to everyone but you three."

Chance sighed. "I really love her but I don't understand sharing her."

"What's to understand? You love her. Jaris loves her. She loves you both. Everyone knows that. What's the problem?"

"I'm not from Destiny."

"Too bad for you. It's the best place on the planet."

"I'm coming to see that, but I was raised to believe that a marriage was between one man and one woman."

Dylan laughed. "So you're against same-sex marriages?"

"Cracking jokes isn't like you." Chance had never heard Dylan act this way before. The guy was so serious and to the point most of the time.

"Erica is teaching me to take myself less seriously. Plus, I'm just trying to lighten you up, buddy. You're quite intense this morning."

"I guess I am. Of course I'm fine with same-sex marriage. But that, too, is between two individuals, not three."

"Really? Have you never heard of the Three Musketeers?"

He grinned. "We're going to have to put you on stage, Dylan."

"No way. These jokes are all for you. I've sort of been in your shoes, Chance. Ready to leave the woman of my dreams."

"You and Erica?"

"Yes. I thought I was doing the right thing. I wanted to leave town and let her and my brother have a life together. I would've made the biggest mistake of my life had I done it. Quit trying to figure it out. Just let it be."

"I want to. I really do, but I'm not sure how."

"I've already told you it's about love. You know what you need?" The humor in Dylan's tone was gone. He was back to his serious self. "You need to be trained as a Dom."

"You sure don't beat around the bush do you? I'm not sure how that will help me in this situation."

"You're being selfish, Chance. Kaylyn is from Destiny. She's not the one with the issue. You are. Your ego is getting in the way. A good Dom knows and understands the needs of the woman he loves. His wants and needs are second to hers. Always. Guess what? Kaylyn wants you and she also wants Jaris. That's what will make her life complete. That's the kind of family she dreamed of when she was young. You want her to be happy?"

"Of course I do, but I'm not sure I'm wired that way."

"Let me set up some training sessions for you and Jaris. We'll get your wiring fixed so that you both can have a future with the woman you love."

Chance took a deep breath. He wasn't sure becoming a Dom would change his mind about sharing her, but Dylan was right. He was being selfish.

Dylan crossed Highway F and continued onto The Narrows, which led up to the Boys Ranch. "What do you say, Chance? Ready to give BDSM a try?"

"Set it up." He hoped Dylan was onto something with the training. Maybe it would work, but he still couldn't imagine continuing to share Kaylyn's heart with anyone, including Jaris.

* * * *

Wearing only his jeans, Jaris walked into the kitchen with Sugar. He could smell fresh coffee mingling with Kaylyn's sweet aroma. "Good, happy, wonderful morning, baby."

"Good, happy, wonderful morning to you, too."

He grabbed her and planted a kiss. Her lips tasted so sweet. "Coffee sure smells good."

"There's still half a pot. I'll get you some."

"I've got it. You just stay right where you are. I'll join you at the table in just a sec." He walked over to the cabinet where she kept the cups.

"Did you hear Chance leave?"

"I did," he answered, pouring his coffee.

"What else did you hear with your Vulcan hearing?"

He returned to the table and sat down next to her. "I heard everything, baby. You okay?"

"I guess so, or do you think I'm crazy?" Her voice held more than a hint of anxiety.

"You're definitely not crazy."

"Is something still bothering Chance about us?"

"It sounded to me like he might have more questions and concerns." Jaris wanted to ease her fears. "But don't worry about that, baby. He'll come around."

"I hope you're right. I just can't figure this out. I know neither of you are from Destiny, but I know we have something very special. Love is love."

"Some say love always wins out."

"That's what I've been taught, but I've seen how long it can take for it to work out. Did you know that Phoebe and the Wolfe brothers were apart for three years even though they were in love?"

"I'd heard that."

"Three years. Crazy. I would die without you and Chance in my life for that long. Hell, for a single day." She took a deep breath. "Are you really okay with us?"

"Absolutely." He grabbed her hand, wrapping his around her delicate fingers. "Honestly, I was a little concerned but willing to try. But after last night and the amazing time we had together, it's what I want, too. Chance may not share my genes, but he is my brother. You are the woman of both our hearts. I'm in love with you and so is he."

"I know he loves me, Jaris, but is that enough for him? I just don't know. How do I make him understand?"

"Baby, it's no longer just you in this fight. We're a family." He knew deep in his heart how true that was. "You. Me. Chance. Family. Together, you and I will help him understand."

Kaylyn leaned over and put her head on his shoulder. "I pray you're right about Chance."

"What time do you have to be onstage today?"

"Not until seven tonight. Why?"

"I have an idea about what we can do to pass the time until we have to leave."

He wanted to keep her distracted while Chance was away. She had so much she was dealing with. The four missing dogs. Potter's outburst. Bayless. But especially Chance.

"I'm up for about anything, Jaris. Should I get dressed?"

He heard her lean back in her chair. "Nope. For what I have in mind for you and me, clothes aren't necessary." He pulled her in close and pressed his mouth to hers, tracing her lush lips with his tongue. Hunger rolled through him for her. *You're mine, Kaylyn. Mine and Chance's.* "Stand up."

"Okay."

He stood, moving in front of her, toe to toe.

"In fact, I want you out of this robe." He tugged on its tie. "Right now."

"Yes, Sir." Her voice shook with apparent excitement.

Standing close to her, he felt the robe fall to the floor. Without hesitation, he cupped her full breasts with his hands.

"May I ask you a question, Jaris?"

Gently kneading her mounds, he answered. "Sure, baby. Ask me anything."

"You know about Phase Four, right?"

"I do." The place was the local BDSM club that many Destonians were members of. "What about it?"

She placed her little hands on the sides of his face. "Have you ever been to that kind of club before? Back in Chicago?"

He knew of two clubs like Phase Four in the Windy City, but was sure there were more. "I'm aware of them, but no. I haven't. Why do you ask? Are you wanting to whip me?"

"Oh no. Not at all. I don't have a dominant bone in my body when it comes to the bedroom, Jaris."

He smiled, knowing she was a little nervous about this discussion. *Let's keep her off balance.* "Really? I bet you would make a very impressive Dominatrix."

"Maybe so, but that's not what I want or need. I have had to be strong to build my dog training school. Did you know I was still a teenager when I got it off the ground?"

He nodded. "Chance told me."

"Don't get me wrong, I'm okay being tough and decisive when it comes to my dogs, but what I really need is to give the reins over to someone else at night and trust them with everything. I swear I'm completely opposite than I am at work when I'm making love."

He ran his hands down her sides, enjoying the feel of her curves. "I know you are, baby. You're soft and tender. A light in a very dark world. But you also have fire. You like excitement and adventure. That's just a few of the things I love about you. So just cut to the chase and tell me what you want." He was already sensing what her answer would be, and that was making his balls grow so very heavy and his cock stir in his jeans.

"I wondered if you would be interested in exploring BDSM with me. You definitely have Dom qualities."

He grabbed her by the wrists. "I do? Name some of them for me."

"A Dom knows himself. He accepts his limitations and understands others have their own shortcomings, too. None of that holds him back. He is open to new ideas and people from all walks of life. He's not a pushover. A Dom's extreme confidence is sometimes misunderstood as arrogance. He is loyal."

Jaris was overwhelmed at how she saw him. "And you think I have all those qualities, Kaylyn?"

"Yes, I do. And more."

He kissed her again, devouring her lips. Knowing she could trust him so utterly despite his blindness overwhelmed him. Holding her made him feel powerful, alive, and strong. "I want to make love to you and you want to spice up the bedroom with a little BDSM play.

Your idea and mine go hand in hand, baby." He bent down and retrieved the tie of the robe. "This will come in handy."

"Yes, Sir. It will." She offered him her hands, placing them on his chest.

He wrapped up her wrists with the cloth strip. "How's that?"

"Perfect. You're a natural."

"And so are you, baby." He lifted her up into his arms. "Come, Sugar."

He carried Kaylyn into the bedroom, his mind running through a variety of things he wanted to try with her. Every wicked thought stoked the burn of desire within him. "Lay down," he commanded Sugar. He heard his dog stretch out on the floor.

He lowered Kaylyn onto the bed and stripped off his jeans. "You have a blindfold for sleeping, Kaylyn?"

"I do. In my nightstand."

He retrieved the blindfold and placed it on her, joining her on the bed. "I want you to *see* me like I *see* you. With your touch." He removed the tie of the robe from her wrists. "*Look* at me, baby." He felt her fingers trace the lines of his face. "Tell me what you *see*?"

"I *see* someone who is strong, Sir. A square jaw. Dimpled cheeks. Manly features. You're a beautiful man."

He ran his fingers over her face, tracing the delicate lines he was familiar with. "And you, baby, are the most gorgeous creature I've ever *seen*." He stroked her long locks. "Your hair is so silky to the touch."

Her hands drifted down his arms. "Your biceps make my mouth water, Sir." Her fingers glided to his pecs. "And your chest takes my breath away. God, you are so muscled."

"And you are so soft." He *gazed* at her breasts again, massaging them gently. "When I *look* at you, I desire to *see* more. I want to touch all of your body, baby. Every inch." He was rock hard, listening to her breathing become more and more labored.

She moved her hands down his torso, circling his belly button. "You have a six-pack abdomen, Sir. Wait. It's an eight-pack."

He traced his fingers down her frame, mirroring how she was touching him. "And you have a tiny little waist, baby. Feels good."

"I want to go lower, Sir. I want to really look at all of you. May I?"

"Be my guest, baby."

He felt her soft hands wander down to his cock. She wrapped one hand around his shaft and the other around his balls.

"I'd like to kiss you there, Sir. If that's okay with you."

"Yes. More than okay." He craved like mad for her sweet mouth to envelop his shaft.

"Let me get on my knees." She slid off the bed. "Will you swing your legs this way, Sir? Please."

"Yes, baby." Once done, he felt her fingers move up and down his legs. With the blindfold on, she clearly still needed to get her bearings.

When her lush lips skated lightly over the head of his dick, he felt his pulse beating hard and hot.

"You taste good. Mmm."

Her pleasure moans drove him wild. "Show me what you can do, baby."

He felt her swallow his cock, creating more heat inside his body, which was already sizzling. He placed his hand on the back of her head. She bobbed up and down his dick. *I'm getting too close. I don't want to come this way. Not today.*

"Slow down, baby."

She didn't. Instead she increased her tempo, sucking even harder on his cock, while squeezing his balls.

"Stop, Kaylyn." He tugged on her hair. "Stop now."

She did, slowly sliding her tender lips off his shaft. The final popping sound that followed told him just how much suction she'd delivered.

"I just wanted to make you proud of me, Sir. I don't want you to leave me." Her voice shook, letting him know how vulnerable she felt.

He pulled her up until they were face-to-face. "Listen to me, baby. I'm never leaving you. I'm never letting you go. I love you. Now that I've found you, there's nothing on earth that can keep us apart. Nothing." He touched her cheek. "Do you understand?"

"Yes, Sir."

"You are mine, Kaylyn Anderson. Mine."

"Yours, Sir." Her breathing was soft and shallow. "I'm yours."

Hearing her admission unearthed an intense primal possessive side of him. He had to claim her. A burning desire consumed him. He'd let her know how much she meant to him with his words, but now he would let her know with his body.

"I'm going to make love to you, baby."

"There's a box of condoms in my nightstand, Sir."

He pulled out a foil package, ripped it open, and rolled the rubber down his shaft. Without a word, he lifted her back onto the bed, and climbed on top of her. His cock pulsed like mad. He shifted his hips until he could feel her slick pussy with the head of his dick. "Mine." With that single syllable, he thrust into her body, taking what was his.

"Y–Yes. Oh. Yes."

He drove deeper and faster, trying to control his lust that had just been primed by her luscious, wet mouth. In and out.

"Jaris. Sir. Yes. Ohhh…yours. I'm yours."

"Mine, baby. And I'm yours, too." In and out. "So close."

She thrashed under him. "Yes. God. Yes. I'm coming, Sir."

He could feel her sweet shivers on his skin.

When he felt her pussy tighten on his shaft, he drove into her one final time, piercing her body with the full length of his cock. Every inch of his body stiffened. "Fuuuck." He released into her, making his ultimate claim.

He rolled to the side, pulling her with him. "I love you, Kaylyn."

"I love you too, Jaris."

Chapter Fifteen

Chance crouched down, petting Sammie. "Good girl."

Overnight, the Lab had delivered her first litter. Six pups, two males and four females, all healthy as could be.

The boys and the Stones had been there to witness the event. They'd just left to go have breakfast and get some sleep.

"She is good, and so are her puppies." Lyle had stayed up all night, making sure nothing went wrong for the new mother or her offspring. "How is Kaylyn doing?"

"Her leg is healing nicely."

"That's good news." Lyle changed Sammie's water. "I'm glad you and Jaris are helping her."

Thinking about how things had been left with Kaylyn made Chance's gut tighten. So much unresolved. He needed to get finished with all his chores and get back to her as quickly as possible. He still wasn't sure how he felt about the kind of relationship she wanted, but that didn't stop him from longing to be with her every moment he was away from her.

Maybe Dylan was right. Maybe being trained as a Dom would help him with his hesitation about sharing her with Jaris.

Lyle yawned. "I might need another cup of coffee."

"You've done enough, buddy. Sammie is going to be fine."

Kaylyn had been trying to convince him to go to veterinarian school, but Lyle, being so shy, hadn't been persuaded. Chance knew he would make an incredible vet. *I think I should join in on Kaylyn's campaign for Lyle.*

"Chance, when do our new clients get to town?"

"The last day of Dragon Week. Sunday afternoon. Everything all set with the new dogs?"

"I guess so. Mr. Bayless got to the ranch with them around eight. I was going to put them with our dogs, but he didn't like that idea. Said he wanted to keep them in their cages last night. They are right behind his truck."

Chance could tell Lyle didn't care for that, and neither did he. Kaylyn's dogs always had the best accommodations—soft beds, heated and cooled rooms out of the weather, and an exit so that they could stretch their legs in a large fenced-off area.

"Where's his truck parked, Lyle?"

"By the RV that Emmett brought here for Bayless. They're both by the big barn." Lyle sighed. "I wish we could delay handing Bayless's dogs over. They need to go through Kaylyn's training."

"They will. Jaris and I will test them Sunday morning before their new owners arrive. Plus, we'll make sure everything meshes for the new owners and their dogs next week during their training together."

"I know. One good thing, those four won't have to stay with Mr. Bayless any longer." Lyle's statement surprised him.

Chance had never heard him say anything bad about anyone before. "There's more to what's troubling you about Bayless than him making his dogs stay in cages outside, isn't there?"

"Yes."

"Aren't the dogs trained like Bayless said?"

"They are trained. I saw him working with them."

"Then what's the matter, Lyle?"

"I don't like the way Mr. Bayless handles them. I saw him kick one of his dogs."

Chance's gut tightened. He patted Annie.

"I don't want that man around Kaylyn's dogs." Lyle might be quiet and shy, but when he did say something, it was best to listen.

"I agree."

"Thanks, Chance." Lyle stood. "Sammie, you take care of your puppies. I'll be back later."

Definitely, I'm joining in the effort to get Lyle to veterinarian school.

"Bye, Annie." Lyle yawned. "I better go check on our other dogs."

"No, Lyle. Amber said she wanted you to come and have some pancakes. Go eat and then go to bed. I'll check on our dogs and then I'll talk to Bayless."

Lyle placed his hand on his shoulder. "Thanks again, Chance. You and Jaris please take good care of Kaylyn."

"We will." Chance got up on his feet. "Come on, Annie."

After making the rounds to check on Kaylyn's dogs, he walked toward the barn where he knew the RV was parked.

He could hear footsteps he'd heard only once before. *Bayless's footsteps.* "Good morning."

"Hello. Miss Anderson with you?"

"No. Doc has strict orders she's not to resume training dogs until she's completely healed. You settled in?"

"I am. You're Chance, right? We met at Miss Anderson's house the other day."

"Yes, I am. Chance Reynolds."

"Pleased to meet you again." The man took his hand and shook it. "The sheriff and the Stones got me this nice RV. I'll be fine."

Something in the man's voice didn't sound right to him. "Good. I have a few questions, Mr. Bayless."

"So do I. What's with all the security around here? I saw this pretty little blonde come out of the house with two bruisers packing heat. I think her name is Belle. She almost looked like their prisoner."

"The two bruisers are her husbands, Shane and Corey Blue. It's a long story, but suffice it to say she needs protection right now."

"Poor thing. Doesn't she ever get a minute to herself?"

"That's none of my business or yours." Chance didn't care for the man. Bayless seemed shady. Was Jaris right to worry about the guy's true intentions? "I want to talk to you about your training methods, Bayless."

"Fuck. Is this about that little prick who saw me with my dogs last night?" Bayless's tone spoke volumes about his anger. "Listen, Chance, I've been training dogs for over twenty years. My methods work just fine. No, they aren't conventional but my results speak for themselves."

"So you pride yourself in kicking dogs, do you?"

"I don't call it pride. I call it a necessity. Those dogs have to know who is boss."

"We have our methods, too. And if we're going to pass your dogs on to our clients, you will follow our rules, understand?"

There was a long pause before Bayless finally answered. "Your school. Your rules. I get it. I'll do what you say. Besides, my dogs are fully trained."

"Maybe so, but they will be tested by us before we pass them off to our clients. So let's get my rules started, Bayless. The first change is we're moving your dogs to our kennels."

"Now hold on, Chance."

"No. There will be no more discussion. Are you in or out?"

"Wait a second. Miss Anderson wants to deliver dogs to her clients. That's what we all want. I'll follow your rules, but I want to keep my dogs close to the RV. You did lose four dogs, didn't you?"

Chance wondered what it would feel like to punch the bastard in the face, but he tamped down his rage. "You want your money. Do as we say or take your dogs and leave."

"Okay. You win." Bayless's words didn't ring true in Chance's ears.

The guy obviously hadn't fully surrendered.

Chance wanted to get finished here and back to Jaris, the one man he trusted more than any other. Jaris needed to know what had happened here and also about Bayless's treatment of his dogs. There was more to his story than the bastard was saying.

"Bayless, let's go get the dogs and take them to their new accommodations."

* * * *

Standing on Kaylyn's porch, Jaris inhaled the pure Colorado air. "This place is quite different from where we came from, isn't it?"

"Very different." Nicole had worked the day shift of the sheriff's security detail, keeping tabs on Kaylyn's house. "Chicago was never this quiet."

"Still isn't." He patted Sugar on the head.

There were those who said a man and woman could never be just friends, but they were wrong. He and Nicole had been friends for years, ever since they'd been assigned as partners back at Chicago PD. Even after Nicole had been sent erroneously to desk duty, they'd remained close. Still were.

"When do you need to leave for town?" She was going to drive them. Good thing, since Nicole was the sheriff's second-in-command.

"Kaylyn is in the shower. She'll take another thirty minutes to finish getting ready. I'd say we should leave in about an hour. That'll get her onstage in plenty of time for the band's mike checks." Thinking about what had happened at last night's performance, his jaw tightened. "What's the latest on Potter?"

"Ethel thought it was best to postpone his trial to next month. The sheriff agreed. We all want him and his buddies as far away from town as possible. There's enough on our plate with the influx of people here for Dragon Week to deal with. Moving the trial to next month is best. Potter and his buddies left town, promising to return to Destiny on the appointed date."

"That's unusual but a good plan." If Potter tried to skip bail, Jaris would definitely join in the hunt to bring the son of a bitch back to town and to justice.

"Jason gave them a police escort all the way to the county line."

The sheriff had gone the extra mile to make sure Potter left the county. Wolfe didn't trust Kaylyn's shooter any more than he did. Potter's apologetic outburst last night hadn't made any sense.

"Would you like me to fix you something to eat, Nicole?"

"Thanks, but no. I don't want to ruin my appetite. I promised my guys that I would have dinner with them at Blue's."

"How are Sawyer and Reed?"

"Doing wonderful. Did you know that we are up to over two hundred head ourselves?"

He laughed. "I never dreamed of you being a cowgirl, but look at you."

"And I'm still an officer of the law."

"Yes, you are."

"And so are you. I'm glad you accepted the sheriff's offer and joined our ranks. We can certainly use you. Plus, it will be like old times."

He heard her voice crack and knew she still had some guilt about the loss of his sight. "Yes it will. I'm happier than I've ever been in my life."

"Sure does seem so. Kaylyn must have a lot to do with that."

He nodded. "I love her, Nicole. She's the best thing that has ever happened to me." He grabbed his former partner's hand. "So you see if I hadn't taken that bullet, I would've never found the woman of my dreams. Don't feel sorry for me and don't feel guilty. This was meant to be."

"Always seeing the silver lining to everything. Same old Jaris." Nicole squeezed his hand back. "I will never give up believing that your sight will return, no matter how slim the chances."

"And you call me positive." He didn't argue with her, not wanting to quell her hopes, but he knew the odds were slim to none of that ever happening.

Jaris heard a vehicle he recognized approaching. By the sound of it, he estimated it to be about two miles away up the road. "We're about to have some visitors."

"We are?"

"The Boys Ranch bus is less than five minutes away."

"Your hearing has certainly improved."

"Not really. Just my focus." *Chance is coming back.* "Nicole, how do your guys make it work?"

"What do you mean?"

"Sharing."

"Ah. My guys are from Destiny. They're brothers. They always imagined a life sharing one woman. Lucky for me, I am that woman. But I'm betting you're asking because you and Chance are both in love with Kaylyn and she wants you both. Am I close to the truth?"

"On the nose, Deputy."

"I'm not sure how to help you. It's easier for me, even though like you and Chance, I'm not from Destiny either. I don't have to share."

"I see your point."

"What I can tell you is a woman can love more than one man. It's very easy for us."

"I know you're right about that. Kaylyn has made it clear that she loves us both."

"Jaris, you and Chance are close. You'll work this out." She took a step off the porch. "I can see the bus now. Cody Stone is driving."

"Chance is with him, right? And I bet so are the boys, since they are the cleanup crew of Dragon Week."

"You're right. I see them." As the bus came to a stop in front of Kaylyn's house, she stepped back on the porch, leaning in close to him. "Are you and Chance both having issues with this?"

"Me? I was concerned about the idea of a polyamorous relationship, but not now. I believe we have something special."

"And what about Chance?"

Jaris heard the bus door open. "Remains to be seen, but I'm not going to give up on him so easily. He loves Kaylyn, and he loves me like a brother." Listening intently, he could tell that Chance and Annie were exiting the bus. "It will work."

"I'm sure you're right."

"Hi, Nicole." Chance's tone seemed softer than it had been this morning when he'd left so quickly. Had he reconsidered everything?

"Hey, Chance." Nicole bent down and patted Chance's companion on the head. "Hi, Annie. Fellas, I'm going to check the perimeter one more time. When you three are ready to head to town, just let me know."

"Thanks, Deputy. For everything." Jaris was glad to have such a good friend in his corner.

"Where's Kaylyn?" Chance asked after Nicole had walked off.

"Getting ready. She should be out in about thirty."

"Good. That'll give you and I time to talk. First I want to talk to you about this Bayless character. Are you sure about his credentials?"

"Jena, Sean, and Matt are still digging into them, but they've found nothing out of the ordinary so far. Why?"

"Something happened at the ranch. The guy is a total prick when it comes to his training style with his dogs. Lyle saw him kick one of his dogs. I confronted Bayless about it and he didn't deny a thing but became very defensive about his methods. The bastard wanted to keep his dogs in cages by the RV that Emmett provided for him, but I put my foot down. Reluctantly, Bayless gave in. His dogs are in our kennels now."

"Fuck, I had a feeling there was something up with Bayless. What about the dogs? Are they trained?"

"Actually, yes. They are very well trained. Lyle and I ran some preliminary testing on them. They passed with flying colors."

"That's one good thing at least. Until we know the full story on Bayless, we need to keep close tabs on him at all times."

"Lyle and the Stones are on it."

"Perfect. Another good thing in our favor is Potter left town this morning." Jaris recounted to Chance what Nicole had said to him about Kaylyn's shooter.

"Maybe Potter and his friends are telling the truth." Chance's tone told him that he was still unsure. "Any sign of our four dogs?"

"No. Jacob Phong and his cousin Josh are still searching. The sheriff had to pull the rest of the team back to security detail for Dragon Week." Jaris was losing hope that Rex, Blue, King, and Rosie would ever be found. Their disappearance remained a mystery.

"I still believe with Lunceford's psychotic obsession and hate of Destiny that the monster is going to make a move during Dragon Week. I know he's gunning for Belle. Shane and Corey will make sure she remains safe. It's our job to make sure the same is true for Kaylyn. I don't want her to get hurt in any crossfire. I want to be with her during the rest of Wolfe Mayhem's performances. Onstage. Jaris, you and I need to stay close to Kaylyn."

"I completely agree." *Time to get straight to the point.* "Have you given any thought to what Kaylyn wants?"

"That's about all I have thought about, buddy." Chance sighed. "Talk about a crazy place. Destiny is like no other."

He grinned. "That's something you can bank on."

"You know about Phase Four, right?"

Jaris couldn't believe his ears. Had Chance picked up on Kaylyn's desire to experience BDSM? "Yes. What about it?"

"Did you know that a big majority of citizens are members of the club? Where else but Destiny?"

"Does that bother you, Chance?"

"Not at all. I just find it unusual. Hell, why should I? The normal family makeup here is not the traditional one man and one woman. Poly relationships are the standard."

"That's true, though there are examples of couples living in Destiny, too."

"Yes, but they are few and far between, just like those who don't practice BDSM."

"No one judges here, Chance. That's what is great about Destiny. Black or white, gay or straight, couple or poly, BDSM or traditional, it doesn't matter here. All are welcome. But you're skirting the issue."

"I guess I am. Don't get me wrong, Jaris. You're like a brother to me. There isn't another man alive who I care more for than you. It's just that sharing Kaylyn was never something I ever dreamed of."

"But you did have dreams of her, didn't you? Lots of dreams. Before you even confessed your true feelings, I could sense them, no matter how silent you were on the topic. Kaylyn, too. She loves you."

"And she loves you. That's the crux of it, isn't it? I talked to Dylan about this on the drive to the ranch this morning. You know he's a card-carrying member of Phase Four, too."

"I do."

"He thinks this whole issue would be solved if you and I got trained as Doms. What do you think about that?"

"I think that's a fantastic idea. Kaylyn and I talked some after you left. She mentioned having desires about the BDSM lifestyle."

"You're kidding?"

"Not at all. Listen, Chance. I know this is hard, but you and I both know Kaylyn is worth it. I don't intend to give her up and I'm sure you don't either. So we've got to work this out together."

The door opened, and Kaylyn joined him and Chance on the porch.

"Hi, baby." He pulled her in close and gave her a kiss.

"Hi, Chance," Kaylyn said sheepishly.

"Come here, sweetheart."

Listening to them embrace, Jaris knew everything was going to turn out just fine. Chance just needed a little more time. He thought about Dylan's suggestion about Dom training. That would be a good first step.

Kaylyn asked, "Are you really okay, Chance?"

"Jaris is right. You're definitely worth everything. This is all new to me. I have a ton of questions and concerns. I can understand how the short term of this kind of relationship works, but it's the long haul that still has me questioning. I'm still not sure about this, but I'm willing to give it a try."

"That's all I need to hear." Kaylyn's tone of hopefulness filled Jaris with warmth. "Whatever questions you and Jaris have, we can figure them out together."

"I know, sweetheart." Chance sighed. "No matter all the answers we discover together, what if it's just not in me for this kind of relationship? What if I am not enough for you? I know if we start down this path, there will be no turning back. And if I still can't find a way to make this work?"

"You will find a way," Kaylyn said. "I know it."

"Sweetheart, you are everything I ever wanted. I don't want to end up hurting you again."

"You may not know it yet, Chance, but you aren't going to hurt me."

"She's right, buddy. The three of us will be a family."

"I hope you both are right."

Jaris could hear the struggle in Chance's tone. "But you will try, right?"

"Yes, buddy. I'll try."

Chapter Sixteen

Kaylyn hit the final high note of one of her favorite songs that Mitchell had written for the band.

The crowd jumped to their feet, applauding like crazy.

Godric leaned over. "You have them in the palm of your hand, love."

"Yes, she does," Big Jim added.

"With pipes like hers, who wouldn't?" Hank was grinning ear to ear.

Mitchell hit the snare, starting the next song in the set. This one, she sang backup, coming in only during the chorus, while Mitchell sang lead.

As Mitchell began the first verse of the song, she glanced over at Chance and Jaris, who were only a step away from her, one on each side. Jaris had made it clear he was more than willing to share her with Chance. *God, I love him.*

I also love Chance. She knew she was walking a fine line with him. Yes, Chance had agreed to give the relationship she dreamed of a try, but he had also made it painfully clear he was still unsure he could make it work for him in the long run.

She came in on the chorus, singing harmony to Mitchell's lead. *"Can't you see I'm the one for you? You hold my heart in your hands."*

Will Chance come around? She couldn't bear losing him again.

"Our love is strong. Our love is true. How do I make you understand how much I need you?"

As Mitchell launched into the second verse, she saw a commotion in the back of the audience. Several of Jason's newly deputized temporary officers were talking to Nicole, who was using her two-way radio.

She looked over at Chance and Jaris and saw they had their radios out, too.

What's happening?

When the song ended, she stepped up to them. "Guys? Is everything okay?"

"No," Chance stated flatly. "Jaris is on the radio with the sheriff now. Listen." He held up his radio so she could hear.

Sheriff Wolfe's voice came through loud and clear. "Their horses came back fifteen minutes ago."

"Whose horses?" she asked Chance.

"Jacob Phong's and his cousin Josh's."

Her gut coiled into a knot. They'd been looking for her four missing dogs.

Jaris spoke into his radio. "Did you find anything out of the ordinary on the horses or their condition, Sheriff?"

"We found blood on one of the saddles. I need all deputies to come to the front of the stage. Patrick, are you on?"

Oh God. No. If anything happened to Jacob or Josh she wouldn't be able to forgive herself.

"Yes, Jason." Mr. O'Learys voice came through. "I'm here."

"We need to cut tonight's activities short."

"I agree. I'll make the announcement now." Without hesitation, Patrick picked up a mike and began addressing the audience. "That's the end of our day, ladies and gentlemen..."

As the dragon expert gave the rest of the announcements about upcoming activities, and the sheriff continued giving instructions to the security detail over the radio, she started trembling.

Chance placed his arm around her shoulder. "Sweetheart, Jaris and I are here. Everything is going to be okay. Don't worry."

"How can I not worry, Chance? Jacob and Josh were looking for our four dogs. I can't bear it if something happened to them during their search."

Mitchell and the other band members came up, asking about what was going on.

Chance filled them in as the crowd began to disperse and Jason's deputies began gathering at the front of the stage.

Jaris came over with Sugar. "Kaylyn?"

"Right here."

He walked to her and pulled her into his arms. "I want to get you home as soon as possible."

"I want that, too."

"Once Jason finishes his briefing, we'll go back to your house."

* * * *

Jaris held Kaylyn tight. The news about Jacob and Josh had stunned all of them. She was trembling and he realized she felt responsible.

Jason came up onstage with Nicole. He gave a more detailed account of the disappearance of Jacob and Josh to those gathered around. Even though Jaris couldn't see the security detail that the sheriff had put together for Dragon Week, he knew them to be quite capable.

"Jacob's dad informed me that they had told him they would return by five," the sheriff said. "No one had been worried when they didn't show up, knowing they were determined to find Kaylyn's missing dogs. But when the horses returned about ten minutes ago without them, that changed the whole equation."

"Sheriff, I'm betting this has something to do with Lunceford," Corey, one of Belle's husbands and a US marshal, stated flatly.

Jaris reached into his coat pocket and touched the handle of his pistol. It was still a talisman that made him feel better in this kind of dire situation, with or without his sight.

"I agree, Marshal," the sheriff said. "This is likely the move we've been expecting. We all want you to keep your wife safe, so you won't be part of the search party. Since Belle is Kip's main target, I also want Emmett, Cody, and Bryant to be excluded, too."

Jaris was impressed with the sheriff's tactical talents. Keeping Amber's three husbands alongside of Belle's two made a great deal of sense.

"We're going to take Belle and Amber back to the ranch after this briefing, Jason," Shane, Belle's other husband and brother to Corey, said. He'd served several years in prison undercover for the CIA, keeping tabs on Lunceford. If anyone knew how the bastard operated, it was Shane.

"I want everyone else to form search parties for our two men."

Easton Black, the leader of Shannon's Elite, the local CIA team, spoke up. "Sheriff, given the seriousness of this situation, I'd like to suggest appointing members of my team as leads so that the search parties will have access to ROCs. You know how spotty cell service can be around here, especially in the mountains."

"What's a ROC?" one of the deputized citizens asked.

"A declassified communication device used by the Agency. Their technical name is Reconnaissance Oscillating Communication Seven Series, but we call them ROCs."

"Great idea, Easton," the sheriff said. "With their range, all the teams should be in constant communication. I'll take a team to Nickel Ridge. Dylan will take another group to Turkey's Pass. Sean and Matt grab a couple of deputies and head down to Narrow Belt. Nicole will be point on this, running the whole operation from my office."

"Sheriff, I'm going, too."

Jaris immediately recognized Hiro Phong's voice. Being Jacob's uncle and Josh's dad, the man had reason to want to be part of the search party.

"Of course. You'll be on Sean and Matt's team, okay?"

"Yes." The tight concern in Hiro's voice was obvious.

"Sheriff, please find my nephew and son." The tone of Melissa, Hiro's wife, was full of a mother's worry.

"We will, Mrs. Phong. I'm sending every man on this one."

"Thank you."

Every man? That meant there wouldn't be men to spare to keep watch on Kaylyn's house. Not good, even with him and Chance acting as her bodyguards.

The sheriff gave a few more instructions and then ended with "Okay everyone, let's get going."

Jaris pulled Kaylyn in close, feeling her trembles increase. "You okay, baby?"

"I'm just so worried about Jacob and Josh. I won't be okay until they are back home safe."

"I know." He kissed her forehead. "We need to get someone to drive us to your house."

"Hold on," Chance said. "I've got an idea. Wouldn't it be better for us to take Kaylyn to the Boys Ranch? Corey and Shane will be there along with the Stone brothers."

"Good thinking, buddy." Jaris continued to be amazed by Chance's insights. "Let's go talk to them about it now."

* * * *

"Lights out, fellas." Holding Annie's lead, Chance stood next to Kaylyn.

He could hear all the boys settling down in their sleeping bags in the basement of the Stone's ranch house. With Lunceford still on the loose, everyone had agreed that moving the boys out of the dorm and into the basement of the big house was the best plan to keep them safe.

Daniel, one of the older boys, said, "Good night, Miss Kaylyn. Mr. Chance."

"Good night, boys." Kaylyn was excellent with all the orphans, always patient and loving. "Close your eyes and go to sleep."

They headed back up the stairs, leaving the door to the basement open.

"Night, Annie," one of the little boys shouted.

Chance grinned, leading Kaylyn to the opposite side of the house to the guest bedroom that Belle and Amber had prepared.

Kaylyn squeezed his hand. "How long before Jaris's shift ends?"

Jaris was pulling guard duty with Shane. Corey had suggested all the men rotate shifts every two hours, walking the perimeter around the property.

Chance punched the button on his watch.

The digital voice announced, "The time is 11:40 p.m."

"Only twenty minutes, sweetheart."

"When does your shift start?" she asked.

"At 2:00 a.m. with Emmett."

"That works out perfectly."

Chance realized what she meant by that. She wanted to talk. Maybe that would be a good thing, since she was obviously still shaken about the news of Jacob and Josh's disappearance.

Sharing her does have at least one thing that appeals to me.

Whenever she needed comforting, he would have Jaris to help with that. But there were more things about the Destiny kind of relationship that intrigued him. Making love to her had also been surprisingly enjoyable, though awkward at first. Would it be awkward again? Maybe.

His mind spun with more pros and cons of it all.

Now isn't the time to try to figure out if I can make what she's asking of Jaris and me work for the long haul. Especially not with Jacob and Josh still missing.

Shane and Corey both had ROCs, so they were in constant communication with the sheriff and all the search parties. The bad news was there had been no sign of the two men yet.

"We're here." She opened the door and walked into the bedroom.

He and Annie followed behind.

Kaylyn started laughing.

"Down, Annie." He turned toward Kaylyn. "What's so funny, sweetheart?"

"Amber and Belle." Her sweet giggles filled him with joy. "They are too much."

"What did they do?"

"There are two cots set up for you and Jaris."

"Seriously?" Chance chuckled. "I'm surprised. I thought everyone in town knew our business. It is the Destiny way. I guess I was wrong. Amber and Belle aren't quite sure what our situation is after all."

Kaylyn stopped laughing. "And *who* is sure of our situation? Not me, and definitely not you."

Damn it, I sure put my foot in my mouth on that one.

He heard her sit down on the bed. "Everything is going to hell because of me."

"Honey, that's not true." He moved onto the bed, putting his arms around her and pulling her in close. "I agreed to try. Remember? We don't need to dive back into the discussion about you, Jaris, and me right now. You're exhausted. You just need some sleep. We all do."

"Sleep isn't going to change one damn thing, Chance. And you're wrong. I am to blame for screwing things up between us and for so much more, too. I've made mistakes, over and over, one after another. When will I learn? I should've set up my four dogs training in a better place, closer to the ranch house. If I had then Potter wouldn't have shot me, and Rex, King, Blue, and Rosie would be in their kennels right now."

Like him, she was realizing the possibility that their dogs weren't going to be found.

She leaned her head into his shoulder. "Lyle told me about Bayless kicking his dogs."

"Sweetheart, I only held that news from you because I wanted you to stay focused on getting better."

"I know. You're always so protective of me. I love you for it." She sighed. "Having to deal with Bayless is also my fault. We wouldn't need the creep's help if I hadn't screwed up. Jacob and Josh are missing because they were looking for my dogs." Her voice and body were shaking, but she continued on. "Worst of all, I've screwed up our relationship. How long did you and I suffer in silence about our misunderstanding about the kiss under the mistletoe? Years. What happened when you finally told me how you really felt? I told you that I was in love with Jaris. I fucked up everything. I know you are willing to try…for me. With all my heart I want both you and Jaris. I'm afraid, Chance. But what if you're right? What if it won't work out? What if you can't…can't…God, I will die if I lose you again."

She began sobbing in his arms, leaning her head into his chest.

Her suffering was killing him.

I guess now is the time to figure things out. She needs me to.

He brought his fingers up to her face and felt her tears. Her overwhelming fear and pain sliced into him like a hot knife. Dylan's earlier words of advice filled his mind.

"You're being selfish, Chance. Kaylyn is from Destiny. She's not the one with the issue. You are. Your ego is getting in the way."

Dylan was right. He was being selfish.

"Kaylyn wants you and she also wants Jaris. That's what will make her life complete. That's the kind of family she dreamed of when she was young."

The former Navy SEAL had spoken the truth and now he was able to see it.

Jaris had been right, too. *"Blindness comes in all kinds of shades."*

Kaylyn had been courageous, confessing her love of Jaris.

What did I do when she opened up her heart? I pushed her away, and I nearly lost her again.

Suddenly, everything seemed clear to him. Jaris was his brother. Kaylyn was the woman of *their* dreams. *We are a family.*

"Shhh, sweetheart. I'm here. I'm not going anywhere."

Her tears seemed to subside. "You're really not going anywhere?"

"No." He heard the familiar footsteps of Jaris, his best friend, his brother, and the man he would share Kaylyn with for the rest of his life.

"Down, Sugar." Jaris's tone was serious. "What's going on, Chance? Why has Kaylyn been crying?"

"Because I've been so blind, Jaris. I've been a fool. No more. I see clearly now. She's all I want. Her happiness is what matters to me, and I know she needs us both. Hell, man. I need you. You're my brother."

"And you're my brother, too." Jaris stepped forward and placed his hand on his shoulder. "We can do this, buddy. We can make her happy."

"Yes we can and will. I'm all in." He turned to Kaylyn. "Sweetheart, no more hesitation. No more doubts."

"You've made me so happy." Kaylyn wrapped her arms around his neck.

"He's all in, baby," Jaris said. "We're family."

"Yes, we are." Chance touched her cheeks, finding the tears he'd caused. "You are ours, sweetheart. Mine and Jaris's."

"I love you, Chance."

"I love you and want to be with you forever."

Chapter Seventeen

Chance realized his life with Kaylyn and Jaris was just beginning. The future had never looked brighter.

He leaned forward, pressing his mouth to Kaylyn's sweet lips. He could feel her surrendering to his kiss. Her breathing softened.

This was her dream and now it is Jaris's and mine, too. This is our reality. Our future.

He released her mouth. "No more doubts, Kaylyn. None. I love you with every fiber of my being. You are my world."

"I love you, Chance, with all my heart." Her words filled him with absolute joy.

"You're my world, too, baby." Jaris stepped forward, sitting on the bed on the other side of her.

"And you're mine."

Jaris kissed her, and she moaned into him. "I love you."

"I love you, too."

"Chance is all in, baby. I told you it would work out. We're a real family now."

Her sweet voice was filled with lightness and happiness. "I am yours, and you both are mine."

"Jaris is my brother. I respect and love him." He wanted to make one thing perfectly clear to her. "There's no other man on this planet I would be willing to share you with but him. Sweetheart, I'm not entirely sure how the day-to-day poly thing works, but I do know that there will be no other men welcome in our family." Chance addressed Jaris. "You agree with me on that?"

"Hell yeah, I agree," Jaris said. "You and no one else, Chance. She belongs to us."

Chance touched her cheek, loving the feel of her soft skin. "Kaylyn, do you understand what we're saying?"

"I do. You and Jaris only." Her voice told him that she welcomed their possessiveness. "You two are all I want or will ever want. I love you. I love you so much it overwhelms me."

"We're about to show you what being overwhelmed by us really feels like, baby." He ran his fingers through her hair. "Aren't we, Jaris?"

"Damn right, we are." Jaris reached into the pocket of his Levi's. "I've got protection. Here's one for you."

Chance reached out and took the foil package.

"What's the other little package for, Jaris?" Kaylyn asked sounding extremely excited.

"It's lubricant, baby. I'd like to send my cock into your pretty ass. Would that be okay with you?"

"I've never had anal sex before," she confessed in a low tone. "But I would like to try. In fact, I'm tingling all over just thinking about it."

Chance pressed his mouth to her lush lips, going deeper than before, becoming more intense. He moved his tongue past her lips, and she wrapped her arms around his neck. Feeling her melt into him, he relished the taste of her surrender.

"Shouldn't we get undressed, guys?"

"Is our girl in a hurry?" Jaris laughed. "Give me those lips."

As he and Kaylyn kissed, Chance ran his hands over her arms, loving the feel of her soft, silky skin. Her little passion trembles drove him wild.

After Jaris ended his kiss with Kaylyn, Chance took his place, devouring her mouth once again. His balls became so heavy and his cock grew. "I can't get enough of your delicious lips, sweetheart."

He pulled her blouse over her head and tossed it to the floor. Together, he and Jaris removed her bra.

"I want to enjoy your gorgeous breasts, baby." He reached out and touched her full mounds. Kaylyn moaned as he lightly pinched her nipples.

"Chance, may I look at your chest? And yours, too, Jaris?"

Without a word, he ripped off his shirt. He grabbed her wrists and brought her delicate hands to his chest. He released her, allowing her to move her fingers over his torso freely.

"God, you are so incredibly beautiful, Chance."

He grinned. "I've never been called 'beautiful' before, sweetheart."

"Get used to it because you are, and I plan on reminding you of it for the rest of my life." She removed one of her hands, and he realized she was touching Jaris with it. "And you are beautiful, too, Jaris. Both of you have the bodies of Greek gods. I've never seen such perfect muscles on any man before."

Chance loved hearing her breathless words. She circled his nipple with her fingertip. He bent down and circled one of her nipples with his tongue.

"Feels good." She clawed at his chest.

When he tightened his teeth around her taut, little berry, he heard Jaris kissing her on the neck. There was something so natural about sharing her with him, something so right. He could tell that Kaylyn's desires were multiplying fast, thanks to his and Jaris's joint touches and kisses. He and Jaris were in complete sync with how and when to touch her, caress her, kiss her.

"Let's place her down between us, Chance."

"Good idea." He helped her to the center of the bed.

"I want to get her out of the rest of her clothes so I can enjoy that little bottom," Jaris said in a tone full of desire.

"And I want to get a good *look* at her sweet pussy."

Kaylyn giggled, obviously enjoying the wicked talk. "And to make it fair, you two need to strip out of your jeans."

"You've got a deal, sweetheart." He and Jaris removed their Levi's, and then pulled off her jeans.

In a flash, he and Jaris joined her on the bed, placing her between them.

"Face Chance, baby. I'm serious about wanting to enjoy your ass."

"Keep talking to me like that, Sir, and you'll get whatever you want."

Chance chuckled. "I think our girl likes to please."

"And she also likes a firm hand."

He heard Jaris slap her ass, and the moan that followed told him that they were both right. *As soon as possible, Jaris and I need to go in for Dom training.* He knew she would love it when they did.

* * * *

Kaylyn's ass stung deliciously from Jaris's slap. Her body burned from head to toe with want.

She gazed at Chance. Though he could not see, his eyes were a beautiful chocolate brown, and his lashes were the longest she'd ever seen on a man.

While kissing her on the back of the neck, Jaris caressed her bottom, spreading her cheeks.

Chance moved his hand down to her pussy. "She's soaked for us, Jaris."

His fingers threaded through her swollen folds, increasing the pressure inside her.

"I can tell. Her scent is driving me crazy."

Kaylyn trembled with delight, hearing their inner beasts come out in both of them.

"Got to have a taste." Chance shifted down the bed until his mouth was less than an inch from her pussy.

She ran her fingers through his hair, wrapping her leg around his back. She held on, trying to steady herself but never quite succeeding. She was slipping fast into a swirl of desire from their intimate touches.

When Chance ran his tongue over her pussy, she felt Jaris begin applying lubricant to her anus. "Oh my God. This feels so good."

Chance circled his tongue around her clit, making her crazy. "Tastes so good."

Her lips vibrated fast as he lapped up her juices. Jaris sent a finger into her ass, stretching her anus. The sting lasted only a second before morphing into an urgent desire.

Her pussy ached and her clit throbbed. "I need you both in me now. Please."

"Yes, baby," Jaris said. "I've got to get inside you. I want to feel your pretty ass squeezing my dick."

"And I want to slide my cock into your tight pussy." Chance shifted back up the bed, rolling on his back and pulling her on top of him.

She grabbed his thick, monstrous shaft and guided him into her pussy. "Yes. Ohhh."

Jaris crawled on top of her, positioning his massive cock right at the entrance to her ass. She bit her lower lip as he slipped past her anus and slowly into her.

She panted as they stretched her out more than she'd ever been before. They reached places inside her body that had never been touched. When they were fully seated in her pussy and ass, they took deep, manly breaths and began moving in sync with deepening strokes into her body.

"You feel so good." Chance's words came from deep in his chest, every syllable blistering hot. He was on the edge of release.

Feeling his cock hit that pleasure spot inside her pussy, she was, too.

Her men thrust in and out of her body, and she felt the immense pressure inside her explode as she squeezed down on both their cocks. "Yes. God. Yes."

Jaris's hot breath blasted on her neck, his exhalations sounding a lot like growls. "I'm going to come."

She writhed between them as her orgasmic sensations rolled through her, drowning her in shivers and tingles.

Chance thrust into her deeply, his body stiffening. "Fuuuck."

"Ahhh." Jaris did the same from behind.

Her body accepted their final release, tightening even harder on their shafts. Her pussy's spasms sparked all her nerve endings, searing every inch of her inside and out.

Her guys rolled her onto her side, each remaining on one side of her.

She stayed locked in their arms for some time. She listened, noticing that even Chance and Jaris's breathing was in sync.

She shivered softly, enjoying the feel of their bodies next to her.

Chance gently kissed her. "Oh my God. That was fantastic."

"You can say that again." Jaris stroked her hair. "That blew my mind."

She smiled. "You were so together in your lovemaking. Amazing."

"That was a first for me." Chance touched her on the cheek.

Jaris laughed. "Then you can call me a beginner, too."

"A first for me too, guys. Not just anal sex. Having two men at the same time. I'm glad my first was with you."

Jaris kissed her shoulder. "You can't imagine how much that pleases me, baby."

"Me too, bro. I love that we were her first."

"Beginners or not, you both sure knew what you were doing. I've never felt anything like this before."

"A new beginning for our lives together." Jaris ran his hand down her sides.

Chance *looked* at her, running his fingers over her face. "A new beginning for our love to grow."

"And a new beginning for our sex education together." She giggled, enjoying the afterglow with Chance and Jaris.

Chance smiled. "I love you, sweetheart."

"And I love you."

"I love you, baby, but I think we could all enjoy a shower together."

"You read my mind, Sir."

Chapter Eighteen

Kaylyn walked out of the guest bedroom's bathroom just as Jaris returned with Sugar from his latest shift of guard duty.

Chance sat up in the bed and yawned. "What time is it?"

"Go back to sleep," she answered. "It's just after eight."

"Yes, it is. And daylight is burning." Jaris laughed. "You planning on getting up any time soon, buddy? The whole house is up. Even the boys are almost done with their chores."

"Don't pick on him, Jaris. Remember he only got back from his last shift at four this morning. He's exhausted."

Jaris pulled her in close. "Guard duty wasn't the only thing that took away our sleep, baby."

"I would gladly give up sleep for the remainder of my life to have more nights like last night with you, sweetheart." Chance swung his legs off the bed and Annie came up beside him.

"Since you are determined to get up. I really would like to go see my dogs and get a look at Sammie's new puppies. Lyle told me that they are adorable. Plus, I need to assess Bayless's dogs. If they aren't up to my standard, I will have to call our clients to delay them coming here."

"Honey, you can't." Chance stood, pulling on his jeans and T-shirt. "Don't forget Doc's orders."

Jaris nodded. "One week. That's all. You've got to be patient."

"I'm just going to take a look and I'm not training. And you both know that I'm always in control of those dogs."

"But you don't know Bayless's dogs, sweetheart." Chance came up beside her and Jaris. "With his type of training they are likely unpredictable. You need to wait."

"That's exactly why I'm going. I am not taking any chances with our clients. You both are great dog trainers, but I'm the one who has been doing this for years. I'm the expert. I don't want any of our clients getting hurt because of your overprotective stubbornness. Now if you want to go with me, that will be fine, but I am going."

"Sounds like you're the stubborn one to me, baby." Jaris turned to Chance. "But she's right. She is the expert."

"Okay, but you will stay close to me and Jaris, understand?"

"My pleasure."

Chance smiled. "Before we head to the kennels, we're going to the kitchen for coffee."

"Good idea, buddy. We both know how she gets when she doesn't have her coffee in the morning."

"Oh, is that right?" She folded her arms over her chest. Then she laughed, realizing that neither of them could see her defiant gesture. "Like Chance has ever let me miss my coffee in the morning."

"I think I'll fill up a thermos for all of us." Chance opened the door. "We might need more than a single cup."

"Excellent idea," Jaris said. "It's unusually chilly this morning."

After getting their coffee, they headed out to the kennels, passing Bayless's RV. There was no sign of the man anywhere.

Corey and Bryant, the current men on guard duty, walked over to them.

"Good morning, guys," she said.

"Morning," they answered in unison.

"Any word on Jacob or Josh yet?"

Bryant shook his head.

"The team isn't giving up," Corey said. "Jason has reached out to other agencies. More men should be arriving later today to help with the search."

She could see the concern on Corey's face and knew it wasn't just about the two missing men. Belle, his and Shane's wife, was still Lunceford's main target. Her bone marrow matched the killer's, who was battling leukemia.

"Where are you three headed?" Corey asked.

"To see my dogs and Sammie's new pups. I also want to get a look at Bayless's dogs. Have you guys seen Bayless around this morning?"

"No. We talked with Lyle. He said the man left during his shift a little after four this morning." Corey's tone was all US marshal. Serious. To the point.

"Did Bayless say where he was headed?" Jaris clearly didn't trust the man despite his credentials panning out.

"Lyle asked him where he was going," Corey answered. "Bayless only said he had business to attend to and would be back later today."

She took a deep breath. Knowing how poorly the man treated his dogs, she would be happy if he never returned.

"Kaylyn, I look forward to hearing you sing again." Bryant, Amber's husband, always did try to lighten the mood when things turned grim. "When does your band perform next?"

"Not this evening, Bryant, but Wolfe Mayhem is scheduled to perform at the closing ceremonies of Dragon Week tomorrow night." She knew that might get canceled given all that was happening. The entire town was stretched to the max with searching for Jacob and Josh, trying to keep security for Dragon Week, and with having to deal with the ongoing threat of Lunceford. "Please let us know if you hear anything about Jacob and Josh, okay?"

"Sure thing." Corey patted the side of his jacket. "We're all carrying our ROCs, so we'll let you know as soon as we hear. How's your leg, Kaylyn?"

"Much better. You can hardly tell I ever got shot thanks to Doc's great handiwork. Stitches will be coming out in a few days."

Jaris squeezed her hand. "Potter will pay for shooting you, accident or not."

"Good thing the judge moved their trial to next month so that he and his buddies could leave town on bail," Corey said. "We have enough to deal with in Destiny without having to keep track of those fuckers."

"We need to get back to our shift duty," Bryant said. "We're going to help Emmett and Cody gather up the boys and get them back in the house."

Corey's face tightened. "I suggest you three hurry with your visit to the kennels and then get back in the house, too. We are considering this a high-alert time until we find Jacob and Josh."

"I promise I won't be long." Kaylyn headed to the kennels with Jaris and Chance and their two wonderful service dogs. Sugar and Annie were two of her best. She hoped, despite Bayless's awful training methods, his dogs would be ready to be handed over to her clients.

After seeing Sammie and her new puppies and all the other dogs, they walked over to the area Chance had placed Bayless's four in and found Lyle working with them. They were beautiful dogs. All male German shepherds—one solid black like Sugar, two black and tan like Annie, and one white.

Lyle looked up. "Morning."

He was a dear friend and loved dogs as much as she did.

She smiled. "Good morning. How's the training going?"

"Haven't had to train them at all. I don't care for Bayless, but I believe you'll see his dogs meet our standards in every way."

"Run them through some exercises. I would but Doc's orders are I can only watch."

"Glad to, boss."

She always found it funny when Lyle called her that since he was like her little brother.

As Lyle demonstrated some commands to the dogs, she couldn't put her finger on what was troubling her about them. They were obeying every word and assisting him the way a service dog was supposed to, but in her gut she knew something wasn't right.

After finishing the demonstration with the last dog, Lyle placed Winter, the white German shepherd, back into the pen with the other three.

"How did they do?" Jaris asked.

She sighed. "They are well trained, that's for sure."

"That's great news," Chance said. "We can deliver these dogs to our clients as planned, day after tomorrow."

Lyle came up, showing two thumbs up. "We're good?"

She shook her head. "No, Lyle. We are not good."

Chance put his arm around her shoulder. "Honey, I thought you said they were well trained."

"I did. They didn't miss a single command. They seemed totally attentive for Lyle, like any good service dog would be. But there's something off with them." She thought about Bayless kicking the poor things and felt her stomach tighten. "I'm not sure what it is, but until I get a chance to work with them myself, they won't be going to any of our clients. We need to get back to the house. I need to call them right away."

Chapter Nineteen

Jaris walked into the house with Kaylyn and Chance, hearing Shane talking to the sheriff on his ROC. By the shuffling of shoes and boots, he knew that all the Stones and Blues were also gathered in the room.

"They found them," Belle whispered to his left. "Jacob and Josh. They're injured but alive."

"Do we know what happened?" Chance asked.

Emmett answered, "Shane is talking with Jason about that right now."

"...ambushed close to the southern border of the county line near Elderkin Lake, not far from Narrow Belt." The sheriff's voice was coming through loud and clear. "Someone shot at them and their horses were spooked, throwing them into a ravine. Dr. Strong says the horses are fine. They just need cooling down."

Kaylyn moved next to Jaris, grabbing him by the arm. "Shane, ask the sheriff how bad Jacob and Josh are hurt?"

Shane relayed the question.

"Doc and Paris are here on scene," the sheriff said. "Jacob's arm is broken and Josh has a gash on his face. Doc says it's nothing serious. Where's Kaylyn, Shane?"

"She's here now."

"Tell her Jacob and Josh found her missing dogs. They are alive and well."

"Oh my God. I can't believe it." Kaylyn hugged Jaris, and he pulled her in close. He was as relieved as she was.

The sheriff continued, "Sean and Matt are bringing her dogs to the ranch now. They were in cages near Elderkin Lake."

"Who the hell was keeping them in cages?" Shane asked.

"Seems it was Potter and his cronies."

Potter. Jaris's gut tightened.

"After the bastard made his false apology to Kaylyn at Dragon Week, Jacob followed the man all the way to his vehicle to make sure he didn't start anything. When Jacob and Josh came upon an empty white truck next to some pens holding Kaylyn's dogs, Jacob thought the vehicle might have been Potter's. When he saw the license plate, he knew for sure it was Potter's. Before he and Josh could dismount, they were fired upon."

Jena's voice came through Shane's ROC. "Sheriff, I've got an update you need to hear."

"Go ahead," the sheriff said.

"I'm at TBK headquarters. You were right to ask me to check the credentials of Potter's attorneys. Turns out the two scumbags are mob lawyers, working for the Russian syndicate, and in particular Anton Mitrofanov. Once I found that out, it was easy to uncover the connection with Potter and the other men. I dug a little deeper and found a few lines of code hidden in their medical credentials that had Lunceford's signature digital fingerprints all over them. Potter and his friends are all on Mitrofanov's payroll. Not Russian mobsters but paid mercenaries."

"Good work, Jena. I already put out an APB on those bastards. I'll be sure to add your findings to it. Whatever Lunceford's plan was, it looks like we're ahead of him this time."

"I hope so," Jena said. "Sheriff, is Jaris with you?"

"No."

"He's with me," Shane said. "He can hear you, Jena."

"This isn't about Lunceford or Potter, but I wanted to let him know I did find out something on Bayless's background he might find interesting."

Shane handed Jaris the ROC.

"What did you find, Jena?" Jaris was glad to have someone as talented as Jena as a friend. "False credentials?"

"No. Bayless is legit. He has a dog training school. That's a fact."

"So what else did you find?"

"Bayless was brought up on charges several years ago for heading up a dog fighting ring in Mississippi. The charges were dismissed on a technicality."

Rage rolled through him. Treating dogs that way was cruel beyond words.

Kaylyn and Chance came up beside him, clearly just as angry about what they'd learned as he was.

Jaris gripped the ROC with his hand, trying to keep calm. "Thanks, Jena. We needed to know that."

"There's more. Bayless filed for bankruptcy a few months ago. He's about to lose everything, including his dog training school. He's not here with his four dogs just to help Kaylyn out of the generosity of his heart. He's here for money and I wouldn't doubt to also try to steal her clients."

"Where is Bayless now?" the sheriff asked.

"He's not here." Jaris squeezed Kaylyn's hand. He knew she was upset by all they'd just learned about Bayless. "Lyle saw him leave early this morning. He didn't say where he was going but did tell him he would be back sometime today."

"Jaris, when Bayless returns, hold him there. I'll send Nicole up to talk to him. I'm thinking there's more to the story than just dog fighting."

"I agree." Jaris hadn't ever met a better lawman in his life than Jason Wolfe. "When Bayless returns, Chance and I will make sure he stays put until Nicole arrives."

"Great. Dylan, are you on?"

Dylan's voice came over the speaker. "Here, Sheriff."

Jaris handed the device back to Shane.

"We'll wrap things up here where we found the guys in about thirty minutes. My team will head back to Destiny. Nicole, how are things in town?"

"Quiet. No rush to get back. Finish what you need to do. I've got two citizen deputies out patrolling the area. We've got a few hours before today's Dragon Week events get underway."

"Good. Let's have all the search parties convene at my office in an hour." The sheriff continued giving instructions about where all the officers would report.

Chance came up and in a low tone said, "Dragon Week is still going on."

"Two more days of it. There's a lot to cover." Jaris didn't envy the sheriff's current situation. Jason had quite the job to do. "Potter is missing. Lunceford is still on the loose. And then there is Bayless to deal with."

"The coordination is critical to make sure everyone stays safe." Chance was dead on.

"I'm sure the sheriff has it under control."

"With everyone's help, yes."

"Sean, are you at the Boys Ranch yet?" the sheriff asked.

Sean's voice came on. "Just pulling through the gate. We'll take them to Kaylyn's kennels."

Jaris could hear an engine off in the distance. Then he heard something he hadn't heard since leaving Chicago. A helicopter.

"You hear that, Jaris?" Chance had clearly heard it, too.

"Yes. I'm betting it's the state's response to the sheriff's APB."

"That was fast."

"They might've had someone close in the area." A stroke of luck they could certainly use right now.

"Guys, let's go get our dogs." Kaylyn was tugging on his arm. "I want to make sure they are okay."

He and Chance walked out the door with her, leaving the rest to listen to the sheriff's assignments. Sugar and Annie led the way.

"We'll have to get Dr. Strong to check them out as soon as possible," Chance said as they walked to the back of the property to the kennels.

"Absolutely," Kaylyn said. The excitement in her voice could not be missed. "Lyle can access their health until then."

Just as they got there, Sean drove up and parked by the building.

He and Matt got out of the truck. They had their ROCs with them, which were broadcasting the sheriff's briefing, which was still going on.

Jaris could also hear the four dogs barking with excitement, Rex being the loudest.

Kaylyn ran to them.

"They're in great condition, Kaylyn," Matt said, opening the tailgate of the truck.

Jaris could feel Sugar's tail hitting his leg. She was excited to see her friends. So was he. He bent down and petted them. He recognized Rosie first. She was the one who loved to lick his hand the most.

"Just look at them," Kaylyn said. "Aren't they so beautiful?"

"They sure are," Chance said. "But I can feel they need a good brushing, especially Blue."

"You're right about that." As happy as Kaylyn clearly was, it was obvious she was also angry for what Potter had done to their dogs. "King has stickers all in his coat."

"Sheriff, we have shots fired in town." Nicole's anxious voice came through Sean and Matt's ROCs. "It sounds like all hell is breaking loose."

"All teams return to Destiny immediately," the sheriff ordered.

Lunceford's attacking.

"We need to get the dogs inside," Chance said.

"Here, Jaris. This way you can stay in touch." Sean handed him his ROC. "Matt and I will head back to town."

Gunshots rang out from the front of the Stone's house.

They all flattened out on the ground.

Lunceford's attack isn't just in town. It's here, too.

All the dogs were snarling, ready to help.

He gave the command to Sugar to get down and stay alert. Chance did the same with Annie and Kaylyn the same with the other four.

"The war has begun," Matt whispered. "Who is inside?"

"Shane, Corey, and the Stones," Kaylyn answered as shots continued to ring out. "Plus, Amber and Belle."

"Sheriff, we have shots here, too," Shane's voice came through. "We've spotted, six…correction eight armed men near the tree line of our fence."

"The house is between us and the shooters," Jaris said, feeling his pulse burn hot. He needed to protect Kaylyn. That was all that was on his mind now.

Shane continued, "Amber and Belle are taking the boys to the basement."

"Belle's the one Lunceford wants," Sean said.

Nicole's voice came through again. "We have a man down in the park. There's also been an explosion at the courthouse."

"We're on our way, Nicole," the sheriff said. "Shane, can you handle your situation?"

"So far, yes. We're holding them off."

"Chance, Kaylyn, and I will get the dogs secured." Jaris reached in and touched his pistol talisman. "You two go around to the side to see if you can flank the attackers."

"On it," the two men said in unison, rushing off.

"Stay low to the ground." Jaris listened intently, in case any of the attackers made it past the house. So far, it sounded like Shane and the other men were keeping the bastards at bay."

The three of them inched their way with the dogs to the building, which would give them more cover. Once inside, they shut the doors.

More troubling updates were coming through the ROC. "Fire at the clinic." "Three shooters outside Blue's Diner." "We have two more officers down."

"We've got to do something," Kaylyn said frantically.

"You need to stay put," Chance said firmly, mirroring his exact thoughts. "You're safe here."

"But what about Belle?"

Jaris put his arm around her. "Even though Lunceford's war is in full swing, with only eight shooters here at the ranch, I'm sure Shane and the other men will prevail."

He heard one of the kennel gates open in the back, and knew it came from where Bayless's dogs were being kept. Had Bayless returned?

"Jaris, how long do we wait?" Kaylyn asked. "Surely there's something we can do to help."

He heard Bayless and his dogs heading their direction, but he wasn't alone. Was Lyle with him? He couldn't identify the footsteps of the other man because of the gunshots being fired outside.

"Baby, the odds here are in our favor." Jaris wasn't so sure about the odds in town. He said a silent prayer for Destiny and for his friend Nicole.

"The odds are not quite in your favor, Detective Simmons," a voice he didn't recognize said.

His gut clenched. *Not Bayless. Not Lyle.* "Who are you?"

"It's Lunceford," Kaylyn whispered.

"Pleasure, Miss Anderson. I guess you've seen pictures of me. No wonder. I am the most notable person in your crummy little town."

Reaching into his pocket for his gun, Jaris heard Chance pull Kaylyn closer to him. He gently tugged on Sugar's lead, sending the silent command to remain on guard.

"It's good to finally *see* you in person, Mr. Simmons. I'm sorry you can't return the favor." Lunceford's voice had a sickening tone. "No pun intended."

"How do you know me? We've never met." Jaris wanted to keep him talking to stall the psycho. Every tick of the clock he could gain from the bastard might prove to be an advantage.

"I knew your former partner, Patti. We met through a mutual business partner who is now deceased."

"Niklaus Mitrofanov."

"You know of him?"

"Yes."

"Ah, of course you do. I must apologize for Patti's mistake. She was supposed to take out Nicole Flowers, not you."

"You're behind that shooting?" Jaris felt rage roll through him. "I'm blind because of you."

"In a roundabout way, Detective, I'm behind everything that goes on in Destiny. That's part of my game. I love games, don't you?"

The shooting outside wasn't letting up. They needed more time.

Keep him talking. Build trust. "Why do you hate Destiny so much, Kip?"

"Actually, I really love the town. They're such good players. With the tiniest of effort, I've built a global organization that has revenues surpassing that of many a third-world country's entire wealth. The only real fun I've ever had is playing with the citizens here. But of course, games must all come to an end sometime. Enough of this chitchat. I've come to get Belle White. She's my salvation. She's my big win. My checkmate."

"You'll never get her, Lunceford." Kaylyn's defiance burned hot in every word.

The monster laughed. "I love Destiny women. They have so much sass. Megan, my ex, must fit in really nice."

"That's why you started attacking Destiny, isn't it? You wanted to punish your ex-wife?"

"No. The Knight brothers were the reason in the beginning. But now it's only about the game."

Jaris listened intently, trying to figure out where the fucker was standing. Holding on to his gun, he kept it in his pocket. Being blind, he hadn't shot it in over a year. But if he could empty all its bullets in

Lunceford and Bayless's direction, there was a slim chance he might hit one or both of them.

Keep the bastard talking. "What's your next move, Kip?"

"No more moves after today. God, I will hate to see this game end. It has been so much fun. One more move left, and then it is good-bye to Destiny forever. Bayless, let's go get Miss White."

"No. She's one of ours," Kaylyn spat. "We'll never let you take her."

"I like your fire, Miss Anderson, but it is wasted on me. I want Belle, not the two other donor matches my sister has caged up for me. I want to win. You must understand that. Besides, what can one woman and two blind men do to stop me? Nothing."

"Don't be so sure about that, Lunceford." Chance was doing exactly what Jaris needed him to do. *God, he's got good instincts.*

"Could you elaborate?" Kip's arrogance came through his singsong tone.

"Like you said, they are good players."

With Chance trying to get Lunceford's attention away from him, he would be able to fire on the bastard and his sidekick creep at the perfect moment.

"Mr. Reynolds. You've been so quiet I forgot you were here. Pleasure, but you're wrong. I have my men creating the distractions that will keep all the players out of my way. By the sounds of things outside, I'm certain most of the Destiny men have left the Stone house to chase the poor disposable pawns."

"Not everyone will leave the house, Lunceford, no matter what you had planned."

"I already thought of that, Mr. Reynolds. Of course Shane and Corey Blue won't leave Belle's side. But with Bayless's dogs, who are trained to kill, I have the advantage."

"Oh my God. That's why you had Potter shoot me and steal my dogs, wasn't it? You bastard."

"Ms. Anderson, you just made my day. Most have trouble seeing the mastery of my plans, but you figured it out in a matter of seconds. Bravo. It gives me an idea."

Jaris heard the helicopter approaching.

"That's our ride, Mr. Lunceford," Bayless said. "We need to hurry."

Not the state's helicopter. Fuck.

"Yes, it is. I want to have Kaylyn as a little extra insurance. She'll be a nice cherry on top of this operation. Bayless, have your dogs take these two out and I'll get Ms. Anderson."

Bayless shouted, "*Dushegubstvo.*"

Jaris jumped up and pulled out his gun, but before he could get off a round, two of Bayless's dogs attacked him and Sugar.

He fell to the ground and hit the cement, jarring his head.

He heard Chance and Kaylyn shout commands to their dogs, which were taking on the killer canines.

She's still okay.

Through the commotion, he tried to concentrate all his attention to locate where Lunceford was positioned.

Need to make my shots count.

Dazed, Jaris blinked several times.

Light and shadows. What the hell?

He shut his eyes and shook his head. He blinked again and gray images began to appear. *Can this really be happening?*

He had believed and accepted that his blindness was going to be permanent, despite the doctors telling him his sight might return. *Am I really beginning to see?*

He concentrated and the shapes sharpened.

My God, will I actually be able to see Kaylyn? My beautiful Kaylyn.

"Kill them all," Lunceford shouted. "I want Belle."

Suddenly, color and images filled his vision.

Lunceford came into focus. He was pointing a pistol at Kaylyn.

Jaris fired his weapon at the monster.

Destiny's villain fell to the ground.

Jaris glanced around and saw Chance had Bayless on the ground by the throat.

Lyle rushed in, hoisting a tranquilizer gun. He fired on the four killer dogs. They all yelped and fell to the ground.

Kaylyn shouted the command for their dogs to back down, and she and Lyle started caring for them.

Jaris ran over to Kaylyn and felt a rush of relief.

She's safe. He ran his hands through her golden spun hair. Her delicate features were fair. She looked up at him with her wide amber-flecked silver-colored eyes. *God, she's so beautiful.*

"Are you okay, sweetheart?"

She nodded. "I am for someone who just went through a warzone. Just a little shook up. How about you? Are you okay, Jaris?"

He ran his fingers over her red lips. "Yes, baby. Knowing you're safe, I am now." He bent down and kissed the woman of his dreams, the woman who had changed everything for him, the woman he would spend the rest of his life with making sure she had everything she ever wanted. He touched her face. "I can't get enough of looking at you, baby. You are so beautiful."

She closed her eyes and brought her hands up to the side of his face. "And you are so handsome."

He kissed her again. "Sweetheart, I'll be right back."

"Okay. Lyle and I need to keep working on our dogs."

Needing to make sure Lunceford was no longer a threat, Jaris rushed with Sugar to where the bastard had fallen.

Sugar was bleeding, but it seemed to be a superficial wound. *Looks like she won the fight.*

Pointing his gun at the psycho, Jaris kicked Lunceford's weapon out of reach of the monster's fingers. Sugar growled at Kip.

The bastard's eyes were wide, but he was still breathing.

Not for long.

Jaris looked at the fatal wound in the motherfucker's chest.

"This isn't possible," Lunceford choked out. "I planned for everything. You can't see."

Jaris leaned over and whispered, "Actually, asshole, even when I was blind, I could see better than you ever could."

Kip rasped out, "This can't be. Please help me."

"But it is, and there is no help for you. It's too late." Jaris thought about all the evil Lunceford had rained down on Destiny. So many had suffered and died at this maniac's hands. Buildings had burned and even the bridge leading into the town had been destroyed. He glanced back at Kaylyn and recalled all the women who had been targeted by Lunceford. She was one of a long list, including Megan, Nicole, Erica, Jena, Phoebe, and Belle. But even through all the hell and deaths, Destiny had survived. Now, the narcissistic psychopath lay at his feet. "How ironic that you will die in the place you tried to destroy, Lunceford."

"I-I…can't die…here…my game…Destiny can't…beat me." The bastard wheezed and gasped for several seconds. The asshole's power was gone. The shock in the killer's fading stare could not be missed. His body convulsed and blood spewed from his mouth as the monster took his final evil breath.

Kip Lunceford was dead.

"Good riddance, motherfucker. You lost. Checkmate."

Jaris ran to help Chance with Bayless. They tied the asshole up with some spare leashes.

The gunfire outside stopped.

He and Chance rushed over to help Kaylyn and Lyle with their dogs.

"You okay, Kaylyn?" Jaris asked her.

"I am now." She was washing out a gash in Blue's coat. "How about you two?"

Jaris kissed her quickly on the lips. "Now that we know you're safe, we're great, sweetheart. I'll check out Rosie."

Chance leaned over and kissed her on the cheek.

Jaris brought the ROC up to his mouth. "Sheriff, can you hear me."

"Go ahead, Jaris."

"Lunceford is dead. He was working with Bayless, who we have tied up here. I'm with Kaylyn, Chance, and Lyle at the kennels."

"Good job, Deputy. That's the best news ever. Shane, how's it going with your situation?"

Shane's voice came through. "We've killed six of the eight shooters and have the other two in custody. Belle, Amber, and the boys are all safe. Not one of our men got shot."

"Same here." Dylan's voice came through. "We took out six of Lunceford thugs by Silver Spoon Bridge."

Jaris pushed the button on the ROC. "Nicole, are you okay?"

"Yes. I'm okay. Jason got to town with the cavalry. We have all of the Russian thugs Lunceford sent to town contained. Twelve dead and six in custody."

"I've got the O'Learys with me. Dragon Week is closed down for today. Hopefully, we can have it up and running for the closing ceremonies tomorrow." Jason Wolfe's voice was full of emotion. "The war with Kip Lunceford is over. We won."

Kaylyn clapped her hands together. "Thank God."

Jaris felt the shared relief spill over from all the voices coming through the ROC.

"We have a lot of work left to do to clean up this mess, but once done, I want all officers and any other interested parties to report to my office first thing in the morning." As the sheriff continued with his debriefing, they went back to work on their dogs.

Chance knelt down, checking Annie out for injuries. "Lyle, how long will the tranquilizers keep Bayless's dogs down?"

"About twenty minutes. I was in the storage room when I heard Lunceford talking to you guys. I loaded up the tranquilizers then."

"Good thinking," Jaris patted the guy on the back. "Let's get them muzzled before they wake up."

Lyle stood and ran to get the muzzles.

"Our dogs held their own with the killer canines, didn't they?" Chance smiled.

Seeing him for the first time, Jaris realized why Kaylyn had been so smitten with him. He was a good-looking guy. "I'm really proud of them." He patted Rosie. "Good girl. You're going to need a few stitches. That's all."

Lyle returned with the muzzles and began putting them on the killer canines.

"I am so proud of all our dogs." Kaylyn was working on Rex.

"Me too, baby." Jaris turned his attention to King. "Could you hand me the pair of scissors by your left leg? I need to cut out some of Rosie's hair around her wound."

"Sure thing." Kaylyn reached for them and then froze in place. "Wait. What did you just say, Jaris?"

"I need the scissors."

After muzzling one of Bayless's dogs, Lyle turned to him. "You said what?"

"Seriously, I don't understand what's troubling you and Kaylyn. I just want the scissors."

Chance smiled. "Jaris, you asked Kaylyn to hand you the scissors by her left leg, right?"

"Yes. Have you all gone crazy?"

"How did you know the scissors were by her left leg?"

"Because...I can...see. Yes, I can see. My God, I can see." He turned to Kaylyn. "You're so beautiful. You're gorgeous. You're the prettiest thing I've ever seen. But I knew you were. I already *gazed* at you with my fingertips."

Kaylyn wrapped her arms around him. "Jaris, I'm so happy. This is a miracle."

"We needed a miracle." Chance grinned. "We always knew there was a possibility of your sight returning."

"Like winning the lottery. I guess when Bayless's dog jumped me and I hit my head, it was all I needed to get my vision back."

Chance laughed. "If I'd known that was all it would take, I would've hit you upside the head a long time ago."

"I know you would've, buddy."

"When I realized you were shooting at Lunceford, I thought you were pulling a Hail Mary, so I jumped Bayless. Little did I know your sight had returned."

Kaylyn released him. "Okay. You can see. Tell me what I'm doing right now." She stuck out her tongue.

"Is that an offer for a kiss, baby?"

Chapter Twenty

Sheriff Jason Wolfe had moved this morning's meeting to Ethel O'Leary's courtroom. Thankfully, the explosion yesterday at the courthouse had been in the parking lot, so the building had suffered no damage.

Jaris walked into the crowded room with Kaylyn and Chance. They'd kept his recovered vision secret. Kaylyn, being Kaylyn, wanted to make an announcement about it after today's meeting. She wanted the whole town to celebrate the surprise together.

Currently, the only four people who knew he was no longer blind were Kaylyn, Lyle, Chance, and himself.

Jaris held Sugar's lead and Chance held Annie's. Dr. Strong had examined them and all the dogs, including Bayless's, last night.

"Have a seat everyone." Ethel stood behind her desk, wearing her robes.

Just like Jaris had imagined, the eighty-year-old was a regal-looking woman. Quite the lady.

"You see any open seats?" Chance asked.

He looked around the room and saw Nicole sitting with her two men, who he'd only seen once—right before Patti had shot him. Beside the trio were three empty seats.

Nicole had always been pretty back in Chicago, but here in Destiny between her husbands and wearing a simple dress, she looked radiant.

"Follow me," he said, taking Kaylyn, the most beautiful woman in the room, by the hand. "These seats taken?"

"Hi Jaris," Nicole said. "They are yours."

He took a seat. "It's nice to see you out of uniform for a change, Deputy. You look nice in that dress."

She smiled back. "Thanks, Jaris."

He grinned, knowing she hadn't realized he could see.

Sheriff Jason Wolfe took the microphone. "Thank you all for being here. I know it's been a hectic couple of days. You may have noticed that Judge O'Leary is in her robes. The reason is we got started early this morning getting our prisoners indicted."

The crowd applauded. Even though everyone was exhausted, they were in a celebratory mood for winning the war on their town.

"The man who shot Kaylyn and his cronies are in custody as well as more than a dozen of Lunceford's other men."

"That's right," someone on the left side of the room shouted. "And Jaris Simmons killed the bastard. Kip Lunceford is dead."

The crowd came to their feet, cheering. "Jaris. Jaris. Jaris."

"Let's bring the man of the hour up here," Patrick O'Leary said. "We want to hear from him."

Kaylyn squeezed his hand. "Go. They won't take no for an answer."

"Only if you and Chance come with me."

"Okay."

They went up to the front and stood by the sheriff, who was smiling broadly.

"Jaris, tell us what happened in the kennels."

He recounted the events, leaving out the part about his sight returning. Kaylyn had wanted to be the one to tell that little detail.

"Hold on, Jaris Lee Simmons." Nicole stood up and left her seat, running to him. She wrapped her arms around him, tears in her eyes.

"What's the matter, Deputy?" the sheriff asked.

"He saw I was wearing a dress."

The sheriff's eyebrows shot up. "And? You ran down here crying for that?"

"Yes." Nicole looked him in the eye. "You can see. Your sight is back, isn't it?"

He smiled. "Yes. It is. Sure took you a while to figure it out, Deputy."

Everyone in the courtroom roared with joy.

Nicole hugged him again and then Kaylyn. "I'm so happy for you."

"I'm happy for all of us," Kaylyn said.

Chance leaned over. "I guess Nicole ruined your surprise, sweetheart."

"If anyone else had spilled the beans I would've been disappointed." Kaylyn grabbed Nicole's hands. "I know you have been carrying a ton of guilt, so I'm thrilled you were the one to let everyone know our good news. Besides, isn't that what's the most important thing? Jaris has his sight back."

Chance slapped him on the back. "You lucky devil."

Jaris had been so wrapped up in all the excitement, he hadn't thought about how Chance would feel. His best friend was still blind.

I've got to talk to Chance.

* * * *

Chance finished his beer. "How about another?"

"I'm empty, too," Jaris said. "I'll get us a couple more."

Kaylyn was in the bathroom getting ready for tonight's final performance.

"Here you go." Jaris placed a can in his hand. "You know, Chance, you're a handsome motherfucker."

He laughed. "So I've been told a million times. But thanks anyway." The can was nice and cold. He popped the top, and took a swig. "God, that's good."

Jaris opened his can. "We deserve some beers, buddy."

"Yes, we do. I still can't believe Kaylyn was able to convince Dr. Strong and Sheriff Wolfe to not put down Bayless's dogs. They were both concerned about the safety of the boys."

"She can be convincing, as you and I both know."

"I think we better take Dylan's advice and get trained as Doms."

Jaris chuckled. "Agreed. Plus, our girl has made it very clear she wants to experience that lifestyle. Truthfully, it has an appeal to me, too."

"Same here. How long do you think it'll take us to rehabilitate Bayless's dogs?"

"Not sure, but with Lyle and Kaylyn working with them, I'm betting it won't be long. We're going to have to be very careful until then."

Chance recalled how Bayless had provided them all the commands for his dogs, which were all Russian words, after some friendly persuasion. "I don't speak Russian. And I don't know anyone else that does. Do you?"

"Not a soul, but until Kaylyn is satisfied they are safe, we'll need to keep them on short leashes." Chance reached down and patted Annie. Kaylyn wasn't about to ever place Bayless's dogs with any of their clients. "They're going to be permanent fixtures here, so I'm sure we're going to get to know them very well."

"They don't know it, but they are very lucky dogs. If Lyle hadn't shot them with tranquilizers, I think our dogs would've taken them down."

"I agree. I still can't believe Bayless's confession about why he wanted Rex, Blue, King, and Rosie."

"Fucking asshole had Lunceford's men keep them in cages because he thought he could retrain them to kill. Guess who's in a cage now?"

"I'm glad we only have to delay giving our four to their new owners for a couple of weeks."

"Me, too. Dr. Strong swears they will all be healed up and ready to go by then. I think the town should give our four dogs medals, Chance. And Sugar and Annie, too."

"I agree. And you too, Jaris. Damn, buddy. You're the hero of Destiny."

"I'm not a hero." Jaris's tone was somber. "We all worked together to beat Lunceford. The real heroes are the two citizen deputies who lost their lives."

"This town will never forget their sacrifice."

"I don't think any of us will forget."

"What's bothering you, Jaris? I can hear it in your voice."

"I'm sorry, man, that you can't get your sight back."

"Don't be sorry for me. How can I miss something I've never had? But you, bro, you lost something extremely valuable but you never complained. Not one person I ever taught learned as fast as you. I've never experienced such determination before. Do you realize what this means to us and Kaylyn? Our training will be so much better as you have experienced blindness. Now that you can see, your help will be beyond measure. Plus, for me I can see so much more than ever before with you and Kaylyn explaining what things look like. Do you remember when she described the clouds looking like big puffy bales of cotton floating in the sky?"

"I do."

"Well, I'm expecting you—a man who knows what it means to be blind—to join her in describing the world to me." He put his arm around Jaris. "I love you, bro."

"I love you too, buddy."

"Our life with Kaylyn is perfect, and our future will be unbelievable."

Chapter Twenty-One

Chance placed his satchel on the bed. He heard Jaris do the same with his.

"How was your first night of Dom class?" Kaylyn's excited tone thrilled him.

He pulled her in close. "Good."

"What did you learn?"

"Baby, why do you ask?" Jaris came up behind Kaylyn, pinning her between them.

Chance liked how in sync he and Jaris always were, especially when it came to Kaylyn, their woman.

"I don't know. I thought maybe you could show me a few things tonight."

"Sweetheart, we've got a lot to learn before then."

"Well at least tell me what's in those satchels. You got them at the club, didn't you?"

"We did," Jaris answered. "But what's inside is something you are going to have to wait to find out. We want to surprise you."

She giggled. "When we go to the club together?"

"Yes."

"Can we go now? The club is open until four."

He and Jaris laughed.

"Our girl is anxious, isn't she, Chance?"

"Definitely. No, sweetheart. Not tonight."

"Tomorrow then?"

Chance brought his fingers up to her gorgeous face. "Not tomorrow or the next day. We have much to learn. We talked to Mr.

Gold." Gold was the owner of the club and was the one training all the new Doms. In his and Jaris's class there were three other men. "He is going to fast track us so that we can be certified as Doms by your birthday."

She wrapped her delicate hands around his neck. "My birthday? That's over two months away."

"Actually, it's exactly two months from today." He kissed her, loving the taste of her lips. "I love you."

"I love you, too, but I think two months is way too long."

"Well, you're going to have to learn to be patient because that's how long it is going to be. But that doesn't mean we can't enjoy some very hot vanilla sex tonight."

"Yes, Sir. Please, Sir."

"I love you, baby." Jaris turned her around.

Chance heard him kiss her and smiled. His hesitation about this relationship was long gone. Now he couldn't imagine not sharing Kaylyn with Jaris. This was meant to be. They were family.

"I love you, too, Master Jaris."

"Listen to her, Chance. Answering you in sweet sub words. You know she's just trying to push our buttons so she can get a peek into our satchels."

"We know how to get her mind off of them, don't we? Time to push her buttons."

* * * *

Kaylyn vibrated with excitement as she slipped on the red leather mini Jaris and Chance had chosen for her for tonight's induction into Phase Four. Jaris liked its color and Chance loved how it felt. It certainly didn't leave much to the imagination.

They'd been taking classes for aspiring Doms, three nights a week. What normally took nearly a year for most had taken her guys only two months.

Two months. God, it seemed like a lifetime ago. A lot had changed in the past sixty days.

Lunceford had died, and the whole town had taken a giant communal sigh of relief.

The closing ceremonies of Dragon Week had gone off without any issues. All the psycho's men, including Bayless, were either in prison or awaiting trial. At long last, peace had returned to Destiny. Last month's big event had been the wedding of Phoebe Blue to the Wolfe Brothers, and though most attendees still carried their weapons, no one had to look over their shoulders for some gunman to jump out.

With help from the O'Learys and some legal maneuvering, she'd been able to acquire the rest of Bayless's dogs, which totaled twenty-two. Unlike the four, who had been trained to kill, the rest were in various levels of training to be service dogs. Six of them were going to be placed next month with new clients.

She reached down and petted Winter, the white German shepherd who had been in the kennel the day Lunceford died. "How's my sweet girl?"

Winter wagged her tail. She and the other three dogs Bayless had trained to attack had been fully rehabilitated. She, Chance, Jaris, and Lyle had worked with them nearly day and night.

She sighed, knowing there were only a few more weeks until Lyle would be leaving Destiny. It was going to be hard not having him around, but she was thrilled he was finally going to vet school. How long had she tried to convince him he was smart enough? It had taken another voice to get him to believe it.

Dr. Mark Strong, who had moved to Destiny less than a year ago after his graduation, had been a major factor in Lyle's decision. Those two had bonded over the past two months and were as close as brothers. Lyle would be taking the other three Bayless dogs with him to Fort Collins.

She heard the door open, pulling her from her thoughts.

Wearing nothing but his biker boots, leather pants, and harness, Jaris walked into the bedroom with Sugar. He looked so unbelievably sexy. The ink on his left arm only enhanced his beauty. He'd designed the image for him and Chance, who sported the same tat on his left arm, to represent their commitment to her. She gazed at it, thrilled that they'd marked their bodies with the image of two wolves, one gray and one black, surrounding a winged angel.

It had taken some convincing, but they'd agreed to let her ink her body with the same image, though a smaller version of it on her right shoulder.

"You about ready, birthday girl?"

"Almost." She'd moved to the Boys Ranch permanently to be with him and Chance. *My men.* With the help of Lucas, an architect and the sheriff's brother, her guys' bedrooms and the kitchen and one bath had been combined into a cute apartment by taking out just a few walls.

"Better hurry. Chance is threatening to leave without us."

"Really? Who's going to drive him?"

Jaris smiled. "He says that since I drove your car while I was still without sight, he thought he might give it a go."

She recalled why Jaris had driven. She'd been injured. "That was different. That was an emergency."

Jaris pulled her in close and kissed her lightly. "According to him, if you don't hurry up, this will merit emergency status."

"Five minutes more. That's all."

"I'll let him know." Jaris walked back to the door, placing his hand on the knob. He turned around, fixing his stare on her. "But if you're not out by then, there's no telling what that crazy man will do. It'll all be on you, Kaylyn."

"Yes, Sir. I promise. Five minutes. I just want to make sure I look good for tonight. This is the first time we've been to Phase Four together. I want to make you proud."

"Baby, you look incredible. Gorgeous. And besides, you can't imagine how proud Chance and I are that you are ours."

He didn't wait for a response, but left, closing the door behind him.

She turned back to the mirror, gazing at her reflection. She'd put her hair up, as they'd instructed her to do for tonight's fun. The black ribbon around her throat had been Chance's idea. She loved how it looked around her neck.

What did Chance and Jaris have in store for her? She had a few guesses, but they were only guesses. Not knowing actually had her jittery and excited. She'd begged them for some lessons at home about what they'd learned during their Dom classes, but they'd refused, saying they wanted to wait until her birthday to unleash their new skills. So, they'd kept their lovemaking with her vanilla. Of course, they were masters already in the bedroom, giving her multiple orgasms night after night.

Last night, no sex. They'd told her they wanted her to get a good night's sleep so she could fully enjoy her birthday. She'd drifted off in their arms, dreaming of the delights they had in store for her.

The door opened again.

With Annie by his side, Chance stood in the doorway, wearing leathers the same as Jaris. His muscles bulged. She couldn't wait to be conquered tonight by her ebony god.

"Sweetheart, it is time to go." Chance's deep tone was firm.

"Yes, Sir. I'm ready."

Barely able to contain herself on the drive to Phase Four, she knew she'd never been this excited about her birthday—ever.

The five of them—she, Chance and Annie, and Jaris and Sugar—got out of the car. Jaris, though his sight had returned, was never without his canine companion. Jaris opened the trunk and brought out the two satchels. She'd nearly died from curiosity about what they held. Tonight she was going to find out what was inside them. One Jaris kept and the other he handed to Chance.

She walked into the club holding Jaris's and Chance's hands. The lobby area was neat with clean lines. Mr. Gold, the owner of Phase Four, sat behind the reception desk in front of a computer. Behind him was the door into the main area of the club. On it was a sign with the words "Members Only."

He looked up at them. "Good evening."

Jaris released her hand, extending his to Mr. Gold. "Evening."

They shook hands.

Chance gave the forms that they'd already filled out and had her sign days ago to Mr. Gold.

"Looks like everything is in order." Gold typed something into his computer. "All set. It's official. Your submissive is in your care as long as you are in the club." He opened a drawer and handed them a key. "Room seven is set up as you requested."

They left Gold and walked through the door into the club, heading straight to room seven.

When they walked in, she saw there was a bench in the center of the room.

Chance and Jaris commanded Annie and Sugar to lie down.

"Take a seat on the bench," Jaris ordered in a deep, rumbling tone, which made her tingle.

"Yes, Sir." She planted herself on the padded surface and felt the cold from its leather on her ass. *No panties.* That had been another of their rules. She folded her hands in her lap.

He and Chance placed their satchels on one of the four tables that were in the room. With a steady gaze, she watched them empty the bags out onto the metal surface. They had handcuffs, paddles, and crops, dildos, butt plugs, and lubricant. Finally seeing the contents of their satchels, she shivered with delight and nervousness at the same time.

Chance came up to her with a pair of handcuffs. "Baby, get facedown on the bench."

"Yes, Master." There was a face cradle, just like massage tables had, at one end of the thing. She placed her head in it. Staring down at the floor, she saw Chance's leather boots come into view.

"Give me your wrists."

"Yes, Master." She held out her arms.

He placed the metal rings around her wrists.

My first time being restrained by him. That thought made her warm all over.

Jaris removed her mini, pulling it down to her ankles, turning the red leather into another kind of restraint. "This ass is gorgeous, Chance." He slapped her ass once, delivering a sweet little sting. "But I think it will look even prettier in pink. Pink is warm and sweet, Chance."

"I think you're right, buddy. Let's start her out with my paddle."

"The black one with the holes? Great idea."

"Let me show our little sub what it looks like," Chance said with a wicked laugh.

Suddenly, the beastly thing appeared in front of her under the face cradle.

"You think you can take some kisses from my paddle, sweetheart?"

Trembling, she answered. "Yes, Sir."

"Let's start you out with five kisses and see how you do."

The paddle vanished from her sight. She closed her eyes, holding her breath, anticipating the slaps that were about to come.

Instead of a slap, she felt Chance run the paddle gently over her ass. "Tell me what you feel, sweetheart?"

"Yes, Master. It feels smooth and cold."

"Very good. Here comes number one."

She heard him swing the paddle through the air and then felt it crash against her bottom, right in the center of her ass. Its kiss was sharp and hot, sending a pulse of electricity through her body.

"How are you doing, baby?" Jaris asked.

Using the words they'd agreed on for tonight, she answered, "I'm green, Sir."

"Number two, sweetheart," Chance said.

Slap.

The paddle's second kiss landed on her right ass cheek, burning deliciously.

"Number three."

Slap.

Tears welled in her eyes, not from pain but from blissful abandon. She was with her men, her Doms. They were taking her to erotic places she'd never experienced before.

"Number four."

Slap.

Her pussy moistened, and she began grinding into the surface of the bench.

"Last one, sweetheart. Ready?"

"Y–Yes, Master."

Slap.

The final kiss was hotter than any of the others. It seared her ass like a branding iron. *I'm theirs. They are mine.*

"Chance, give me your hand," Jaris said. "I want you to *see* what pink looks like."

She felt them move their fingers over her ass.

"It's a beautiful, warm color. It might be my favorite color on our sub." Chance's lusty, dominant tone made her even wetter.

She felt them apply lubricant to her ass, stretching her out nicely.

Chance ran his hand up her back. "Fuck, you are gorgeous. I'm going to plug your ass with this."

In her field of vision a toy appeared. It was a dark blue and so very big.

"Sweetheart," Chance said. "I want to get your pretty ass ready for my cock."

"Yes, Sir. Please, Master. Please."

"Take a deep breath for me."

She obeyed.

"Let it all out."

When the last ounce of air left her lungs, he shoved the toy into her ass. The sensation it gave her was an odd mix of pain and pleasure. In no time the pain was gone, leaving only the feeling of pleasure.

Jaris and Chance flipped her on her back. They'd stripped while she'd been facedown. Their godlike bodies glistened with heat, and their massive cocks were hard. Both her Doms held a sex toy—Jaris a vibrator and Chance a violet wand. Both her Doms were smiling wickedly, which increased the pressure that was building inside her.

They removed her top and bra. She was completely naked now, still restrained by their handcuffs and by her mini at her ankles.

Chance ran the electric device over her nipples, kissing her with its warm sparks.

Jaris turned on the vibrator and placed it on her pussy.

"Oh God. Yes. Please. Masters. Please. More. More."

Chance turned up the power on the wand, pressing it to her taut nipples.

Moans passed from her trembling lips, as Jaris sent his toy into her channel.

"Close, Masters. So close."

"Come for us, baby," Jaris whispered, removing the vibrator and pressing his lips to her throbbing clit.

"Yes, sweetheart. Come. Come, now." Chance pressed his mouth to hers, swallowing her moans.

The pressure released, flooding her with warmth and shivers. She clawed at Chance's shoulders and wrapped her legs around Jaris's neck.

Setting aside the vibrator and wand, her Doms quickly took off the handcuffs and removed her mini from her ankles. With the plug still in her ass, they lifted her off the bench and placed her feet on the floor. Her legs were so weak, she had to lean into Chance for support.

Jaris got down on the bench, facing her. "I want to feel your pussy around my cock, sub."

"Yes, Master." With Chance's help, she crawled on top of Jaris.

She could feel the head of Jaris's massive cock on her wet, swollen folds. "You feel so good, Master."

"So do you, baby. So do you." His hands were on the back of her thighs. "Slide down my dick. I want to feel your pussy's grip on me."

She obeyed, taking his inches slowly into her body, relishing the intimate connection they were sharing.

"I'm done with this toy." Chance tapped on the plug, sending a shiver through her. "Sweetheart, I want to feel your pretty ass."

"Yes, Sir. I want that, too." She could barely breathe, as Jaris thrust up into her pussy. But she needed to feel both her men.

Chance removed the plug. She felt him cover the backside of her body with his muscled frame. When the tip of his cock touched her anus, she trembled and the pressure began to build again.

He plunged his cock into her ass, and she screamed, unable to hold back.

In perfect sync, Jaris and Chance began thrusting into her body. In and out. Over and over. Faster and faster. She closed her eyes, writhing between them, in glorious torture.

She screamed again as another orgasm exploded inside her. Spasms ran through her body, as they continued their assault.

"Coming. Fuck." Jaris's eyes closed, and he thrust up into her one last time. She could feel him unload his seed into her body.

"Me, too!" Chance shouted. He pounded into her a few more times before his body stiffened and he, too, came inside her.

Her body shook and writhed into a state of complete satisfaction. She was in the arms of her Doms, her lovers, her men. *Jaris and Chance.*

This is heaven.

Chapter Twenty-Two

The day had turned out perfect for Lyle's send-off party in Central Park. The whole town was there to give him their good wishes and support.

Jaris sat next to Chance. Sugar and Annie were at their feet. Chance's parents and sister were sitting with them, anxiously waiting for Wolfe Mayhem to perform. Kaylyn was standing on the side of the stage.

Lyle was center stage, standing between Ethel, Patrick, and Sam O'Leary.

"We're thrilled to be sending off one of our native sons to veterinary school, Mr. Lyle Tanner." Patrick smiled broadly, placing his arm around Lyle's shoulder. "Dr. Strong, would you please stand up and wave at me so I can see where you are?"

"Over here." The vet was sitting several rows up and to the left.

"As one of Destiny's newest residents, we are thrilled to welcome you, but we are even more grateful you were able to encourage Lyle to take this momentous step."

The crowd applauded.

"Thank you, Dr. Strong." Ethel O'Leary took the mike from Patrick. "My husbands and I also want to show our support to Lyle." She turned to Sam, who handed her an envelope. "Lyle, this is a check to cover all your costs for college—tuition, fees, living expenses."

"Oh my God. I can't believe this. Should I really take this?"

"Yes, son," Sam said. "You need to take it."

Lyle, who was obviously not used to this much attention, hugged the dear lady. "Thank you." He released her and then gave both Patrick and Sam a big group hug. "Thank you so very much. I was planning on working a full-time job. But now I can dedicate all my time to studies. You're making my dreams come true."

"But there's more," Patrick said with a grin, motioning to his left.

Suddenly, a horn started honking. Everyone turned to see a brand-new Ford Mustang driving onto the grass and in front of the stage. Inside were the Knights—Megan, Eric, and Scott. They jumped out and walked up on the stage.

Megan handed him a set of keys. "Lyle, we want you to arrive in style to school."

"Oh my God. This is way too much. Since I lost all my parents by the time I was seventeen, I learned to depend on myself. Now I know I'm not alone. Destiny is my family."

The crowd went crazy.

Lyle hugged the Knights.

"We have more surprises coming up. Wolfe Mayhem is going to play for us. And there will be one more presentation for our guest of honor. Don't forget to enjoy the food that our local restaurant owners have provided. We'll continue our program shortly."

Betty, Kaylyn's mom, who was sitting with her two husbands in the row right in front of him and Chance, wiped her eyes. She loved Lyle like he was her own son.

"Sugar, are you okay?" her husband Harvey asked.

"I'm fine. I'm just so happy." Betty had been thrilled when her two husbands returned to Destiny from Alaska two days earlier than planned. With the dog training school growing so fast, Harvey and Darryl Anderson were leaving their oil field jobs to work with Kaylyn. Betty and her men would never have to be separated again.

Jaris had seen how surprised Chance had been when his family quickly had come around to support his new, unique relationship with him and Kaylyn. Chance's parents were incredible, and his sister,

Paige, was charming as could be. They'd welcomed both him and Kaylyn into their family with open arms.

"How much time before the band starts playing?" Paige asked.

Chance punched the button on his watch.

The digital voice announced, "The time is 11:41 a.m."

"In under twenty minutes."

"That's just enough time." Paige stood. "Mom, would you like me to get you a plate of food?"

Chance's mother shook her head. "I think I'll go with you. There looks to be several booths with all kinds of food to choose from."

All the local restaurants were providing food.

Jaris watched as Jacob, recently out of his cast, helped his uncle and aunt set up Phong's Wok's booth by The Red Dragon statue. Josh was helping the sheriff, Mitchell, and Lucas carry more folding chairs from the courthouse for the crowd.

"I'm coming, too." Chance's father got up on his feet. He was as tall as his son. "I'm getting hungry."

Betty turned around. "Mind if we join you? I'm sure my guys are starving."

Darryl smiled and Harvey nodded. They were good men, the salt of the earth.

"Of course," Chance's mother said. "We're all family now." She turned to him and Chance. "What about you two guys? You want to go with us or have us bring you back some plates?"

"No thanks, Mom. Jaris and I plan on eating with Kaylyn after she finishes her set."

"Okay, but don't give up our seats."

"We won't."

The six of them walked away, leaving him and Chance alone.

"Jaris, can you do me a favor?"

"Anything, buddy."

"Tell me where Kaylyn is. Describe what's she doing and how she looks."

He smiled. "My pleasure. Our girl is walking up onstage. She's wearing a white dress. White is warm and soft, Chance, just like the white in the fluffy cotton bale clouds, which are floating above her now. The wind is lightly blowing her hair. She's looking our way, smiling and waving."

Chance waved back and put his arm around Jaris. "You know we're the two luckiest men in Destiny, don't you?"

"Buddy, we're the luckiest men in the world."

THE END

WWW.CHLOELANG.COM

ABOUT THE AUTHOR

Born in Missouri, I am happy to call Dallas, Texas home, now. Who doesn't love sunshine?

I began devouring romance novels during summers between college semesters as a respite to the rigors of my studies. Soon, my lifelong addiction was born, and to this day, I typically read three or four books every week.

For years, I tried my hand at writing romance stories, but shared them with no one. Understand, I'm really shy. After many months of prodding by friends, authors Sophie Oak and Shayla Black, I finally relented and let them read one. As the prodding turned to gentle shoves, I ultimately did submit something to Siren-BookStrand. The thrill of a life happened for me when I got the word that my book would be published.

I do want to warn the reader that my books are not for the faint of heart, and are strictly for adults. That said, I love erotic romances. Blending the sexual chemistry with the emotional energy between the characters in my books is why I love being a writer.

For all titles by Chloe Lang, please visit
www.bookstrand.com/chloe-lang

Siren Publishing, Inc.
www.SirenPublishing.com

Lightning Source UK Ltd.
Milton Keynes UK
UKOW07f1830200115

244809UK00018B/461/P